John Matthias was born in 1941 in Columbus, Ohio. For many years he taught at the University of Notre Dame, but also spent long periods of time in the UK, both at Cambridge and at his wife's childhood home in Hacheston, Suffolk. He has been a Visiting Fellow in poetry at Clare Hall, Cambridge, and is now a Life Member. Until 2012 he was poetry editor of *Notre Dame Review* and is now Editor at Large. Matthias has published some thirty books of poetry, translation, scholarship, and collaboration. His most recent books are *Kedging* (2007), *Trigons* (2010), *Collected Shorter Poems Vol 2, Collected Longer Poems, Collected Shorter Poems, Vol. 1* (all verse) and *Who Was Cousin Alice? And Other Questions* (2011) (mostly prose). In 1998 Robert Archambeau edited *Word Play Place: Essays on the poetry of John Matthias*, and in 2011 Joe Francis Doerr published a second volume of essays on his work, *The Salt Companion to the Poetry of John Matthias*.

Also by John Matthias

Poetry
Bucyrus (1970)
Turns (1975)
Crossing (1979)
Bathory & Lermontov (1980)
Northern Summer (1984)
A Gathering of Ways (1991)
Swimming at Midnight (1995)
Beltane at Aphelion (1995)
Pages: New Poems & Cuttings (2000)
Working Progress, Working Title (2002)
Swell & Variations on the Song of Songs (2003)
New Selected Poems (2004)
Kedging (2007)
Trigons (2010) *
Collected Shorter Poems, Vol. 2 (2011) *
Collected Longer Poems (2012) *
Collected Shorter Poems, Vol. 1 (2013) *

Translations
Contemporary Swedish Poetry (1980) (with Göran Printz-Påhlson)
Jan Östergren: Rainmaker (1983) (with Göran Printz-Påhlson)
The Battle of Kosovo (1987) (with Vladeta Vučković)
Three-Toed Gull: Selected Poems of Jesper Svenbro (2003)
    (with Lars-Håkan Svensson)

Essays
Reading Old Friends (1992)
Who Was Cousin Alice? and Other Questions (2011) *

Editions
23 Modern British Poets (1971)
Introducing David Jones (1980)
David Jones: Man and Poet (1989)
Selected Works of David Jones (1992)
Notre Dame Review: The First Ten Years (2009) (with William O'Rourke)

An asterisk indicates that the title is published by Shearsman Books.

John Matthias

Different Kinds of Music

(A Few Things about Timothy Westmont)

A Novel

Shearsman Books

Published in the United Kingdom in 2014 by
Shearsman Books Ltd
50 Westons Hill Drive
Emersons Green
BRISTOL
BS16 7DF

Shearsman Books Ltd Registered Office
30—31 St. James Place, Mangotsfield, Bristol BS16 9JB
(this address not for correspondence)

www.shearsman.com

ISBN 978-1-84861-370-6

ACKNOWLEDGEMENTS

Thanks are due to *Boulevard* for publishing 'Westmont and the Bear' and,
as an independent sequence, all of the numbered interchapters under the
title 'Westmont and the Different Kinds of Music.' Thanks are also due to
the web magazine *Flashpoint* for publishing 'Westmont as Talbot Eastmore'
under the title 'Sixth Story.' Early readers of the manuscript-in-progress
were William O'Rourke, James Walton, John Hennessy, Michael Anania,
and Robert Archambeau, all of whom offered good advice.

CONTENTS

i.m. Joel Barkan

The opening eight bars of the second movement of Schubert's Quintet in C major (D. 956, Op. posth. 163), 1828.

Westmont and the Teapot

Timothy Westmont realized that he had managed to get his hand stuck in the teapot. He had taken it down from a high shelf and, as it had not been used for several years, was trying to dust out the inside with a small cloth. Then he found that he couldn't remove his hand. He was entertaining a representative of the neighborhood historic association after a meeting at the City Hall where he had been obliged to argue before a committee chaired by the architectural commissar, one Ms. Angela Copstoner, Ph.D., that the charges against him for having restored his front porch columns with the wrong style of capitals should be dropped. Where there had been Scamozzi capitals before the storm there were now Doric capitals…

…It had all been a very unpleasant business. When the storm blew through the neighborhood Westmont had been on the telephone with his doctor's secretary trying to obtain information about a recent medical test. Suddenly the electricity all went off and there was a terrific crash at the front of the house. The telephone, however, continued working perfectly. The secretary was saying, "You'll be glad to know that test turned out to be completely normal, Mr. Westmont." But Westmont was then shouting at her through the phone as if she had been responsible for what had just happened: "A big fucking tree just fell into my house, and there's a huge limb filling up the entire living room." The secretary said: "Well, there's also a big fucking stain on your chart where I've spilled my coffee, and the doctor would like to see you again in six months."

Westmont put down the phone and surveyed the damage. A formerly tall limb of the large maple tree that had been standing in his front yard was now lying diagonally across his living room. All of the windows were broken and he had actually to climb over the limb in order to reach the door. A neighbor was already waiting there, concerned that Westmont might have been injured when the limb thrust itself through the window. He had not been hurt, he said. He had been on the phone in another room. The neighbor said goodbye—and to let him know if he needed any help cleaning things up.

It was a good deal more complicated than "cleaning things up." When Westmont's wife came home from work she was appalled at the damage and immediately announced that her long delayed trip to see her family in England would begin at once. She was on the phone to a travel agent even before Westmont could find the name of his home insurance company in the phone book. They spent the evening sitting on opposite sides of the great limb in the living room talking about the house and their future together. Sally Westmont thought they needed some time apart. Would Westy mind a whole lot if he were left in charge of house repairs?

While his wife talked on about the things he should do when she was away, Westmont was thinking about the time when he was eight or ten and an oak tree blew down in his back yard in Columbus, Ohio. He and his cousins played for days among the dying leaves, crawling up and down the limbs that jutted out at every imaginable angle into the sky and down into the ravine at the edge of the family property. They pretended they were lost on a capsized ship within sight of an island. "Ahoy, ahoy," they shouted. In the end, men came with saws and cut the capsized ship into firewood, which was stacked in the shed at the end of the yard. His father, who had pushed him on a swing tied to a nearly horizontal limb of the old oak—an experience that was one of Westmont's primal memories—lugged the pieces of wood into the house for years. It kept them warm through many a winter night.

Westmont's wife was packed and gone within forty-eight hours. The Tarkington College steno pool, where she had worked for many years in a clerical capacity, had only recently awarded her some extra vacation time. As the Brandine Construction Company already had men working to realign the front door in its frame, she left by the broken window, Westmont passing the luggage through behind her. "I'll call you from my sister's sometime tomorrow," she said. Westmont sat down miserably on the limb.

During the three days it took before the limb was cut into pieces and removed from his living room, Westmont spent his evenings reading by candlelight. When leaves dropped from the smaller branches, he patiently gathered them up and put them in the trash. When his wife phoned to say she was in London, she said he sounded odd. He felt odd too. None of the downstairs lights in the house were working, he told her, and he was feeling depressed. She said she was sure the electric company would fix things up very soon. She was tired and jet-lagged and going to bed. Hanging up the phone, Westmont again surveyed his domain. He thought about the cost of all the repairs, the negotiations with insurance men. Brandine Construction had only agreed to fix the door and temporarily board up the broken windows until all of the insurance estimates were in and they could make a formal bid. On the second day, while Westmont was out shopping for food, they cut through the tree's great trunk and took away the parts of it that had crashed through his roof and porch. Because he wasn't home and the door was locked securely in its repaired frame and the windows were by then boarded up, they left the limb in his living room. That night he phoned his cousin in Denver. Did Richard remember the time a great tree had fallen down in Columbus and all the cousins played on it for days pretending it was a sinking ship? Richard had no memory of this, but he hoped Westmont was well. They hadn't seen each other for years. They really ought to get together one of these days.

II

Westmont stood before the entirely unsympathetic jury at the City Hall. He had prepared a formal statement and was determined to read it. His wife was leaving him. He had been drinking for weeks. To make matters worse, he had caught a terrible cold from one of the Brandine Company carpenters who had come back to inspect his work on the new columns and smart Doric capitals that had been installed—illegally as it turned out—at their tops. The jury was made up of three Historic Preservation Commission members, two members of the Chamber of Commerce, and his neighborhood representative on the County Council. He had, said Ms. Copstoner, the chief of the Historic Commission's architectural police, replaced and destroyed the original Scamozzi capitals on his house in violation of the new ordinance passed on September 5, 2005. The Scamozzi capitals had been made of local mud and horsehair and dated, the Historic Commission estimated, from the time the house was built, in 1907. Westmont was responding to the charges. The work had cost him $3,000 more than the insurance company had paid Brandine and Company. The Historic Commission argued that the columns must be torn down and authentic replicas of the Scamozzis must replace the Doric capitals. In violation of a recent city ordinance, Westmont would have to pay.

Westmont first said that as far as he was concerned, the so-called Scamozzi capitals were Ionics, but they could agree to disagree on that for the moment. The point was that the story of these repairs went all the way back to the storm in the fall of 2001 when a large tree fell on the left side of the porch at 840 Clark Ave., destroying the ceramic capital on the left column (as one faced the house) and cracking all of the others. He insisted that he must foreground this date because all work on the capitals actually began as a result of the 2001 storm, and all of his subsequent work was a response to that. He understood that he would eventually have to replace all of the capitals, but could only get the insurance to

13

cover one at the time (the one that had crumbled into dust). This was all, of course, before the recent ordinance was passed, as was the start of follow-up work that Joseph Brandine and Co. began doing for him in July, 2004.

Immediately after the storm the entire porch roof had to be restored, beginning in November of 2001, while work on some of the porch, including the capitals, was delayed until spring of 2002. The delay was due to the difficulty of finding an appropriate capital. He could locate nothing Ionic—okay, or Scamozzi—which he could afford until Brandine came up with a ten-inch-diameter plaster replica ($274.00) which was finally installed. The plaster, however, looked nothing like the original clay and horsehair original. It appeared even from a distance to resemble a plastic imitation, a kind of Disneyland version of the real thing, and he disliked it from the beginning. (The source of the plaster imitation was Decorator's Supply Corp., 3610 South Morgan, Chicago.)

All of the other Ionics—Scamozzis—were, as he said, badly damaged. By the summer of 2004 they were porous and disintegrating, letting water into the columns which had begun to rot from the inside out. Joe Brandine began looking for replacements for these in September, 2004; the continuing work of restoration could be said to have begun at that time. Nothing that Brandine was able to find seemed to him satisfactory. He did not want to use the plaster imitations again as he had come to dislike the one previously installed. There was some urgency that the work should get under way, but still he delayed beginning, looking around until the summer of 2005.

As Westmont spoke he slowly began to notice his surroundings. The old radiators hissed and steamed like those he remembered from his elementary school house in the late 1940s. The meeting room, in fact, recalled the school's "Room 100," the largest gathering place in the building, where there were weekly "all school assemblies." This room had even more clanking and steaming radiators than the big classrooms, and he remembered liking to listen to the xylophone music they played and the hiss of the ill-matching pipes and fittings. Mrs. Swales, his fourth grade teacher, would lead the singing: mostly patriotic songs, but also occasionally some rather subversive versions of what she called "folk tunes," which were really written by living contemporaries like Woody Guthrie and Pete Seeger, both banned from the O.S.U. campus during those years. He never wondered in fourth grade if Mrs. Swales was a leftie, but he suddenly wondered now, losing his place in his text.

14

Looking up, he apologized. Sitting at the table in front of him were those officials already indicated, but also an "architectural historian" brought in by Ms. Copstoner. Westmont suddenly noticed that she was quite good-looking. She gazed at him with what he took to be a sympathetic stare. But as he prepared to find his place and go on, he noticed that she had a withered right arm and a kind of baby's hand at the end of it. He tried not to stare at it, but then realized that he had shifted his eyes to her breasts. She must not have been wearing a bra, as he could see her really quite marvelous nipples pressing against a sweater. Her business-like jacket was unbuttoned, dropping straight from her shoulders. The word "deformity" formed on his lips.

The whole of his porch, he said, was deformed. The winter of 2005 was an extremely difficult time for him. His wife had suddenly left for England after the initial storm in 2001. She never returned. Once in England, she took up with an itinerant musician and, in 2005, filed for divorce. He himself had not been well, and he was able to do only those things necessary to get by. He supposed it was at some point in the winter that he missed the discussion of the new ordinance that was passed, he believed, in April of 2005. At any rate, he was unfortunately unaware that forms needed to be filled out for the Historic Preservation Committee if he was going to make any changes in the capitals. If letters, brochures, or other information had been sent to him during this period, he was afraid he hadn't read them. He was focused on a major upheaval in his life, and he might possibly have thrown these missives away, considering them to be "junk mail."

While Joe Brandine continued to look for capital replacements, the existing capitals deteriorated further over the winter. Joe could not find Scamozzi capitals of the correct size. They would need to be made in two halves, in order to fit around the tops of the columns. Full Scamozzi capitals could only be installed by removing columns from the porch and jacking up the porch roof, a complicated and expensive task. In the end, still unaware of the new ordinance, he decided to replace the Scamozzi with Doric capitals. He made this decision, he said, only after looking at all of the other houses up and down Clark Avenue, and especially at the two on either side of him, both of which had Doric capitals. On July 11, 2005, Joe Brandine and Jeff Dierbeck were photographed by the Historic Preservation Society at work on…

…and he realized that the woman with the withered arm and hard nipples was asking him a question. "Mr. Westmont," she asked. "Do you believe in history?"

"What do you mean?" said Westmont, flustered.

"Well," she smiled, "in preserving and honoring the past."

"Of course," he said, "I'm a professional archivist at the college."

"But not on the street?"

"The street?"

"Yes, on your Clark Avenue home turf where you've knocked down one-hundred-year-old Scamozzi capitals made of local mud and horse hair, an exceedingly rare example of typical Queen Ann ornamentation from the period around the turn of the century. In fact, they were the only surviving Scamozzis in the entire Historic District. The abacus was beautifully formed, both the fillet and the cyma reversa, and so were the volute, the embellished echinus with its unique egg-and-dart, the astragal, necking, and flute." And she held up a photograph for all to see.

Westmont, feeling the effects of his cold and wiping his nose with a red handkerchief, hadn't quite taken in what she said. "I don't know about the embellished necking and eggs," he said, "but my own point is that I knew nothing at all about the ordinance until after the work was done. Otherwise, I would, of course, have filled out the forms. "

"Ah," she said. "Ignorance of the law is no excuse."

Westmont went back to his statement. "I was about to mention the pictures," he said. "One of your agents arrived with a camera once the work had begun. I think his name was Dane. This Dane began taking pictures and shouted out to the carpenter that he'd better stop what he was doing. I was inside and did not hear the exchange, so I'm not certain what was said next on either side. But the carpenter got in his car and drove off. The first I learned of the encounter was when Jeffrey Dierbeck of Brandine and Co. phoned me to say that Dane and Ms. Copstoner, who had been lurking under a tree, had frightened off their carpenter by telling him he was in violation of a new city ordinance and would get a subpoena himself to appear before this body if he didn't cease and desist. The weathered harm done to the columns"—but Westmont realized he'd said "withered arm"—and paused. "The weathered harm"—this time he said it correctly—"done to the columns had reached a point when Brandine and Dierbeck believed..."

"This is really all beside the point," Ms. Copstoner said. "The only issue is whether you did or didn't replace the Scamozzis with something else. We even sent you our own estimates and plenty of options available from Classic Tops and Trim as early as September 17th, 2004. We mailed them out to you twice, along with information regarding how you might jack off your roof to install them at absolutely minimum cost."

Westmont blew his nose. He was certain now that he had a fever. And, of course, Ms. Copstoner had said jack up the roof, not jack it off, which is what he thought he had heard. He now began to ramble on about the crisis of his domestic affairs. "You don't really get it," he said. "My wife had left me with a tree in my house. Can you imagine how I felt? She just walked through the window and disappeared from my life. She never liked this country much. She's English, you see. She knows a good deal more than this commission about Queen Anne style, I can tell you. Her brother-in-law's in the House of Lords. You ought to see her beating the members silly in chest. She castles her king and prompts her bishop and knight. If she were here she'd make you ashamed of how you speak the language when even so I'd comply with it in principle. The ordinance. It's just that the work's already done. Moreover, since you've gone and introduced photographs, I'd like to point out you haven't got any pictures of the columns before 1926, twenty years after the house was built. There have been plenty of changes over the years, including the addition of two full rooms at the back of the lot. Scambrozis could have been addled at any point before 1926 say 1925. So maybe at the start there were Dorics. Even so I did give all this a try. After the twelve-inch Tuscan column caps from Classic Stairs and Trim the stuff high-density and molded-plastic wooden at the top additions and we found the porch railing was also in a state and so to reinforce the paint the same kind of time. Please see invoice for the work already done, $2,302.00. Please see also invoice estimate for the cost of taking all that down and doing the Scamozzi over $4,353.00. I am not barbarian or even out of sympathy with general aims of the Historic Preservation Commission. But even under Period Homes website fiberglass—looking nothing like original ceramic—cost-prohibitive. I have spent a great deal of money. When I called my cousin Richard when the tree was in the house he sadly had forgotten how we played a sinking ship on all those limbs and big trunk that fell in the ravine, ahoy, I don't suppose a single one of you has spouse who left you through a window without giving notice or have had to come before a court like this when feeling poorly and ought to be in bed."

Westmont blew his nose and sat down, dizzy.

Ms. Copstoner said that perhaps the commission had enough information and could adjourn until the next week's meeting.

III

He had walked home with the architectural historian. His house was less than a mile from the City Hall, so he hadn't thought to drive. She too lived in the immediate neighborhood and said she was concerned about his health. Having regained his composure after he sat down in the meeting hall, Westmont thought that she was probably even more concerned about his state of mind. Anyway, he had appreciated the company. She seemed a nice enough lady in spite of her having asked him sarcastically during the interrogation if he believed in history "on the street." And she had told him as they walked along that her name was Jennifer Armstrong.

When they reached his front door Westmont was feeling better. Maybe it had been the heat in the County-City building that had made him feel so ill and strange. Anyway, trying to make light of the issue between himself and the organization that Jennifer Armstrong worked for, he had said: "And these are the offending capitals. Doric capitals. Classically austere. I like them." Jennifer had said she liked them too, but that her liking or disliking them had nothing to do with the case against him. He was, she laughed, "a criminal in the eyes of the committee." As they stood rather awkwardly in front of the porch, which was still under repair, Westmont suddenly asked her if she'd like to share a pot of tea. Thanking him for the offer, Jennifer followed Westmont into his house and sat down comfortably on his sofa. At that point Westmont almost immediately made a bad mistake. He said: "And that Copstoner woman! How can you work for such an irascible person."

"Oh, she's not so bad," Jennifer said. "In fact she's my lover." And when Westmont looked embarrassed she said: "You do look embarrassed." She shook the fist of her little hand on her withered arm and repeated: "You do, do, do, Mr. Timothy Westmont, look a little embarrassed." She gave him what the feminists had taught him to think of as a "male gaze."

Westmont awkwardly excused himself and went to his kitchen in order to make the tea. Reaching up to the top shelf, he lifted down his wife's favorite Victorian teapot, which he had not used since she left him but thought Jennifer Armstrong might appreciate. Holding it under his left arm pressed against his side, he took a small dishcloth in his right hand and pushed both the cloth and his hand into the pot. He thought he should dust it out and then give it a good rinsing before putting in the boiling water and loose tea in the English fashion—was it hot water first and then tea? or tea first and then the water?—but soon he was thinking about something else more urgently procedural than the question of whether the water or the tea was first in the pot. He realized that his hand was stuck. Trying to make it as thin as possible inside the pot, he pulled and pulled until he had begun to scrape the skin from the knuckle of his index finger. He tried running a little water from the tap around his wrist, but this made it worse. Then he tried a bit of cooking oil. Then a little butter. Nothing seemed to help, and now the knuckle of his little finger was also skinned and beginning to bleed. He feared he was going to have to ask Jennifer for some assistance.

As he walked into the living room with the teapot dangling from his right hand, Jennifer laughed, he thought, sympathetically. "Oh my, Mr. Westmont," she said, "you seem to have got yourself in a bit of a pickle. Shall I give it a tug?" He held out the hand with the teapot on the end. "But first," she said, "do hold it up in the air for a moment." Westmont did so. "It looks," she said, "rather like a Scamozzi on a somewhat wounded column. Can you hold it even higher? Ah, ha!" she said. "Statue of Liberty now. If you had a hand the size of mine, you could get it in and out without difficulty. You could get, Mr. Westmont, right to the bottom and out again. Perhaps we ought just to leave you like you are. Now let's see…"

But Westmont didn't want to see anything else. He realized at last that he was being mocked. He felt himself to be a victim of aggression. His nose was running badly and he could only wipe it on his sleeve. "What are you up to?" he asked, alarmed.

"Up to? Or down to?" she said. "Always down to business, Mr. Westmont. Always down to business. And you people who don't understand codes. You're always up to trouble. Up to no good. You think you can get away with murder."

"Murder?" he said.

"It comes to that. You've murdered the historic happiness and smiling face of your own front porch. You are, you are…"

But Westmont's landline was ringing in the other room and he trotted in to answer it. It was his cousin Richard in Denver. Richard had called to chat. He said that he had remembered that day when the tree had fallen down in Columbus and how all of the cousins had played on it, just as Westmont had reminded him a while back. He said they were all getting old and he thought it was important to share these things with others who remembered them, and that he was sorry he had forgotten the incident when they spoke about it some years before. He had realized that it was a really great moment in his childhood, part of a childhood idyll he had shared with his brother Robert, and Westmont, and their cousin Jim. He said he had been having this dream…

But Westmont's cell phone was ringing in his jacket pocket. "Richard," he said, "my other phone is ringing, I've got to hang up. I've only got one hand."

"Only got one hand?" said Richard.

"One hand," said Westmont. "I'll call you back."

He managed to get the cell phone out of his left inside pocket with his left hand. Not an easy thing to do. It was his wife phoning from London. She had split up with her boyfriend and was having a hard time. In fact, she was completely broke and wondered if Westmont could manage a small loan. She promised she'd never ask for anything like this again, but things were quite desperate, and it was really urgent. Westmont said he only had one hand and would have to call her back.

She said, "What's happened to you, Westy?"

He said, "There's someone here."

He pressed *disconnect*.

Westmont walked back into the living room with the teapot still dangling from his right hand. "Miss Armstrong?" he said. But there was no one there.

Westmont and the Different Kinds of Music

1

No lullabies that he remembered. Did anyone sing to him? Must have. His mother? Aunt Jean? One grandmother died before his birth, the other senile shortly after. So what music was first? He could only remember from his tricycle days, not from the days when he lay on his back and presumably saw a large something hanging over him that opened and shut. Did it sing? What he remembered was "McNamara's Band." That was his special tricycle music. Round and round the dining room table he'd go until the wind up Victrola wound down. 78 rpms. Big brittle stack of them. He only liked "McNamara's Band" and could find it easily in the stack. He'd wind up the machine, put the rasping needle in the groove, and remount. Pedal pedal pedal then, singing along:

> My name is McNamara, I'm the Leader of the Band,
> And tho' we're small in number we're the best in all the land.
> When the drums go bang, the cymbals clang, the horns will blaze away.
> MacCarthy puffs the ould bassoon while Doyle the pipes will play;
> Oh! Hennessy Tennessy tootles the flute, my word 'tis something grand.
> A credit to Ould Ireland, boys, is McNamara's Band!

He loved it until he hated it. Loved it until he hated it so much that one day he took it off the machine and broke the record over his knee. His mother saw him do it. "Westy," she said. "Why did you do that?" He gave her a startled look and said, "I thought I didn't like it any more."

Westmont at Walloon Lake

Timothy Westmont awoke with a start and was very confused about where he was. He first thought that perhaps he was in Columbus, Ohio, as the trip over there for his mother's funeral had been the first journey away from home he had taken for several years. Then he thought he might be in Saint Louis, as he had recently had some correspondence with an old friend about possibly attending a conference there. But next he heard water lapping and felt a cool breeze on his face. He opened his eyes. There were his various meds: Irbestartan, 150 mg; Simvastatin, 20 mg; Atenolol 50 mg; Escitalopram (generic for Lexapro) 10 mg; Lorazapam, .05 mg; and then some over-the-counter things: Systane for the eyes, Acetasol for the ears. He had also brought along some Viagra, acquired after his wife left him and returned to live in England where she had been born. He had never had occasion to use it and wondered if it actually worked.

He staggered to his feet and found the way to the bathroom. His prostate, he thought, still must be ok, since he had, as he kept telling his doctor, a "vigorous stream." He was way ahead of the medical profession about PSA exams, always having refused to have one. Now, of course, they were generally discouraged for people his age. Even if he did have a bad prostate, something else, statistically, was much more likely to kill him. He shook his dick, then looked at his face in the mirror. He didn't look good. But not bad either. He just needed a shave and a shower. Slowly it came back to him. He was at Walloon Lake, in northern Michigan, and he was here because he had suddenly decided to return to the idyllic site of certain childhood experiences that he remembered with a combination of nostalgia and humiliation. It had been fifty years since he was last at this lake. He had been just a kid, twelve years old. He walked out of the bathroom, through the living room, and onto the front porch. It hadn't been spoiled by developers, this view. In fact, it was just as he remembered it when he had stayed at Shadow Trails Inn so long ago. The lake, the shoreline, the few houses in the village: just the same. Pristine. Quiet. A canoe and a sailing boat were already out on the lake. The sailboat was a "Seventeen," a real beauty. His landlord and neighbor here, Harvey Schach, made and sold these boats. A "Seventeen" was long and narrow, fast, and carried a lot of sail, just right for this particular lake. Westmont knew from the Schach website that Harvey used to be owner of the general store in Walloon Lake village, and also, at one point, the mayor. Being mayor of Walloon Lake village was doubtless a job with very few responsibilities. Owning the general store was more of an obligation.

Westmont realized that he'd better go to the village store himself, and soon. Aside from his pills, he'd brought very little with him. His decision to come up here was totally impulsive, and he realized he hadn't even brought along a windbreaker or a hat. As he certainly intended to do some boating and, over at Lake Michigan ten miles away, some beachcombing for Petoskey stones. He realized he had better drive to the store right away and purchase what he'd need. Then he thought, what the hell, he'd rather walk.

He was a little unclear about where his cabin actually was along the shoreline of Walloon. When he'd been here in the 1950s he had stayed on the southern most point on the lake at Shadow Trails Inn, a lovely rustic lodge with log cabin outbuildings, now unfortunately in private hands. He had gone there the summer he was twelve, two years before his parents had persuaded him to spend two weeks at Tar Hollow Camp in Southern Ohio. He remembered that he had never been able to walk to the village from over there; he would either drive with his father in their 1949 Plymouth or take a boat with his grown-up friend Kevin. Kevin wasn't all that grown up in 1952, but Westmont at the age of twelve found a seventeen year old boy so beyond his own experience that he could only think of him as an adult. Kevin had befriended him a few days after he had arrived with his family at Shadow Trails. "Hi there, Buddy," Kevin had said, smiling from behind the steering wheel of his idling Chris-Craft at the end of the dock that Westmont was about to dive from to swim all alone for the third or fourth time. Westmont had said, "My name's not Buddy," and Kevin had laughed his distinctive swallowed chuckle and then looked serious and asked: "Well then, what's your name?" Timothy Westmont had said, "My name's Timothy Westmont."

"But what are you called?" asked Kevin.

"I'm mostly called Westy by the family, but never at school."

"Well then, Westy, if I may, you can call me Kevin. Would you like a ride in my boat some day? It's very fast. Feel free to join us one afternoon. You always seem to do things by yourself."

A Chris-Craft in the 1950s was the Cadillac of motorboats. Made of gleaming dark wood panels (always polished, always bright), it had a powerful inboard engine with a deep rumble as it idled and the high whine of a Formula One race-car at top speed. Water skiers loved these boats because of their high wake. Sailboats on the lake kept as far from them as possible, and considered them to be objects of new money's vulgar display. Often, as in Kevin's case, their captains flew a variety of flags. U.S. flags. Confederate stars and bars. Jolly Rogers. Yacht-club ensigns. With the engine on idle, the exhaust, low enough on the stern to be under water when even low swells passed by, burbled with a sound like some kind of exotic sea mammal that had just surfaced to spout. Westy stared at the boat and at Kevin in awe.

"I'd love a ride in your boat," he had said. "When can we go?"

"Oh," said Kevin. "My girlfriend's here at the Inn. Everything kind of depends on her schedule."

As Westmont left from the back door of his cabin, he heard someone asking what he liked to be called. It was Harvey Schach, walking toward him from a dry docked boat and smiling. Westmont had found the cabin with a Google search. Within five minutes he'd determined the price, the duration of his stay, and the way to pay for two weeks with a Visa card. But he hadn't yet met Harvey Schach. Harvey was working early on the hull of a Seventeen, and another was parked in the same shady driveway with Westmont's Corolla. When he had arrived the night before, Westmont had admired the elegance of these boats. He knew that Harvey Schach was proud of them since the website on which he'd learned about the cabin was also full of advertisements for them and photographs. They were very expensive. The cabin, however, was reasonable. With a few clicks, Westmont had booked it. Now here was Harvey himself, looking like "The Old Man of the Lake." He had a bad limp, a bald head, and a full gray beard. Westmont guessed he must be at least eighty.

"And you're Mr. Westmont," Harvey said. "You arrived last night when I was at the Country Club, North-East branch of the lake. I didn't want to disturb you when I got home. Is everything okay? It's been a little cold this week, but as you see there's a fireplace and plenty of wood. The chimney draws very well. Did you make a fire?"

"I didn't need a fire," Westmont said. "But I'm glad to know I can make one. I'm off to the village. I think it's up to the end of South Shore Drive and then down the M75 for about half a mile?"

"That's right," said Schach. "But you can also walk along the lake. The path is public access, even though it passes right in front of several front-yard patios. Just brazen it out. The owners or landlords know about the path, but sometimes glower at people walking on it anyway. What shall I call you, Mr. Westmont? Please call me Harvey."

Westmont thought for a moment. "Why don't you call me Westy. It's what I used to be called when I was here before, in 1952."

"1952!" said Harvey. "In 1952 I'd only been coming here from Cleveland for three or four years myself. It was quieter then. No jet skis."

Westmont gave Harvey a wave, and started up the public access path. He could see at once two more Seventeens secured to buoys fifty yards or so out in the lake. There were two docks where the path began, one in front of his cottage and another in front of Harvey's large house. At his own dock there was just a canoe. At Harvey's dock there were a pontoon boat, two kayaks, and a rubber paddle craft. Someone was swimming toward the square stationary platform mounted on flotation barrels twenty yards or so from the end of Harvey's dock.

In 1952 Westmont had thought this kind of platform seemed to be mysteriously suspended from heaven. There was one like it at Shadow Trails Inn. It didn't occur to him that it was probably secured to the murky bottom of the lake by some cable mechanism or other. A day or so after he'd met Kevin, the entire clientele at Shadow Trails Inn was witness to their favorite local's most popular performance. With his girlfriend in the Chris-Craft, Kevin got into his water skis on the floating platform. Then he took up the large triangular handgrip and the rope. Very slowly, his girlfriend brought the rope up out of the water until it was taut in the air. Then she gunned the engine and Kevin appeared to fly. From the floating platform, he sailed into the air for what Westmont thought must be a thousand yards, then dropped onto the surface of the water, crossed first the high wake on the left, then skied back across it and over the wake on the right, kicked a ski, put the hand gear behind his neck, raised both arms in the air, and shouted: "Joy! Joy! Joy!"

Kevin's girlfriend was called Joy.

It took nearly an hour for Westmont to reach the village shop. He was hot and tired when he arrived, but pleased that the shop was just as he'd remembered it. Even the elderly men sitting around the lake-side table with their mugs of coffee seemed the same. At the counter there was a gray-haired lady he judged to be about his own age or maybe a little older. She was reading *The New York Times*. Amused, Westmont asked for coffee and a doughnut, pointed to the *Times* and said, "When I used to come up here as a kid we only had the paper from Petoskey."

"It's in the rack, if you want it," she said indifferently. "Shall I take the coffee and doughnut out to the geezers' table, or is this to go?"

"Geezers' table?"

"It's a tradition with us," she said.

"I'll take it to go," Westmont said. "But I'm also looking for some other things. I hope to do a little boating and I've not got a proper windbreaker or even a hat."

"Clothing store's in Boyne City," she said. "But if you don't mind something that looks a little too much like a souvenir, we've got baseball caps that say *Walloon Lake Village*."

"I'll take one," Westmont said.

As the counter lady led him to another room, Westmont realized that she was still pretty good looking, someone who might have been quite beautiful in her youth. She also walked as if she knew this was the case.

"Here are the caps," she said. "All the same. You just adjust the gizmo at the back."

Westmont noticed that, in fact, he was in a room mainly full of books, which were resting on board-and-brick shelves like the kind he'd built himself when he was a student.

"Are these all yours?" he asked. "Or are they for sale?"

"For loan," she said.

"This is a library?"

"Kind of," she said. "For people we know and like, people who will be kind to the books and bring them back."

At once, Westmont was interested. "I'm an archivist," he said.

"Well, well."

Westmont thought that had sounded a little sarcastic. "It's not a bad job," he said. "As a matter of fact."

"What's in your collection?" she asked.

"Lots of William Faulkner," he said. "We've got a Faulkner scholar at my college who is an avid collector. He's passed a lot of valuable books and manuscripts on to the library's collection. But there's lots of other stuff. Medieval, mostly."

"Have you got any Hemingway? This is Nick Adams country, as you probably know. There's a shop in Horton Bay that's got a bibliographically complete collection, even *Three Stories and Ten Poems*. You might want to stop by."

Westmont remembered about Nick Adams and Walloon Lake. He hadn't read those early stories since his adolescence and he now thought of them as something mainly suitable for young readers.

"I think I grew out of Nick Adams at some point," he said.

"Well, well," the gray-haired lady said a second time. "You know what we're like here," she went on. "We're like the northern Midwest branch of Shakespeare and Company in Paris. At least that's the way I think of it. The shop lent out books long before there was a public library, even back before Harvey Schach owned the store. The new library building is very nice, but it's not much of a collection. Still, we like to know the folks we lend books to."

Westmont was about to say that he was surprised she knew about Shakespeare and Company, but stopped himself and said instead: "Would you be willing to loan books to me? I came up here in a hurry and didn't bring anything along. And by the way, I'm Timothy Westmont."

"I'm Deborah Steinbeck," she said.

"Steinbeck!" he laughed.

"I know, I know." Then she reached down to a low shelf and pulled out a book. "Why don't you borrow this? It's about all the stories set around here, even the strange foolishness of *The Torrents of Spring*. That one's set in Petoskey." She handed him the book: *Hemingway in Michigan*, by Dr. Constance Cappel.

Westmont said: "Why do some people insist on calling themselves Doctor when they don't practice medicine? What's the big deal about a Ph.D?"

"Connie had some difficulty getting hers, so maybe she's proud of it."

For the third time in about ten minutes, Westmont felt a little ashamed of himself. "Do you know the author?" he asked, trying to recover.

"Everyone around here does. She interviewed my father's generation of locals in the 1960s. I met her a couple of times. She was very persistent getting this book into print. Its method was even kind of original when it was published."

"Thanks," said Westmont. "I'll borrow it on your recommendation. May I take a couple of others?

"Browse at your leisure," Deborah Steinbeck said, returning to the front desk to check out a couple of customers.

Westmont looked along the shelves. A lot of the books were only of regional interest, but he could see at once that the shelves were also full of serious literary works. All of Hemingway's contemporaries and mentors were grouped with his own books rather than in alphabetical order. There were Sherwood Anderson, John Dos Passos, Gertrude Stein, Joyce, Fitzgerald, and the other usual suspects, including Steinbeck. There was even a little Faulkner in the old Modern Library editions. Westmont reached down and pulled out *In Our Time* and *The Torrents of Spring*. The copies had been read a lot, and were not in good shape. Someone had not been all that "kind to the books" in the way Deborah required. Nevertheless, Westmont took them all up to the front desk.

"I'll take along these two, as well as Dr. Constance Cappel," he said.

"Just write the titles and your local address in the book." Deborah said, pushing forward a kind of ledger bound in heavy boards. You can have them for two weeks. She was smiling now. The first full smile he'd seen on her rather stern face. "And here's your doughnut and coffee."

Thanking her with a simple nod of his head, Westmont left the shop feeling cheerful, the books under his arm, coffee and doughnut in the small brown bag that Deborah had handed him. He said hello to the old men sitting at the "Geezers' Table" as he passed by, but got no response. It was clear they were arguing about something as their voices had grown louder and louder during the time Westmont was in the shop.

He returned to his cabin by taking the same route back along the house fronts and gardens bordering the public footpath. The wind was whipping up some whitecaps on the lake. If a serious storm came out of this, he knew it would be a result of high wind coming off Lake Michigan, which was only ten miles or so away. Walloon didn't flow into the big lake, but nearby Lake Charlevoix did. Often boats would turn back when they'd passed the narrows between Charlevoix and Michigan and encountered the big waves. When Westmont had been in college his uncle, James Merkel, had made the mistake of sailing out into Lake Michigan on a day like this. His boat had capsized and Uncle Jim had drowned. Another uncle, Bob Jacoby, had been on board. He had managed to hold onto the mast, but Jim was swept away. It took well into the next day to find the body. His uncle had been the first of his parents' generation to die. Westmont's mother, at age ninety-three, was the last. When they phoned him from the nursing home to say that his mother had fallen in her room, there was a snowstorm raging outside. He was urged to drive over to Columbus and take charge of things, but he explained he couldn't even get the car out of the drive. Maybe he could fly out tomorrow. When they got his mother to the hospital, she was found to have not only a broken hip but pneumonia as well. Of course, they couldn't operate on the hip. Within a few hours it was clear that she was dying. He spoke to her once on the phone and she sounded perfectly cheerful, asking about his work. An hour later a nurse phoned and in a very officious way said, "Your mother's pupils are dilating and her nails are pitting. It's what we see." He asked if he could speak to her, but the nurse said: "It's what we see when someone is on the verge of death." There was only one more call before they hauled her body off for cremation. After he put the phone down he turned to tell his wife that his mother had died, forgetting for a moment that his wife was in England.

There was no one to tell.

The whole family had gone to Walloon Lake for the summer of 1952. That meant, as Westmont was an only child, cousins and aunts and uncles. The group was so large that Merkels, Jacobys, and Dawsons filled up the main lodge all by themselves, so the three Westmonts stayed at one of the cabins in the nearby woods. At dinner, everybody got together in the dining room. Westmont enjoyed this at first, but within a few days of first going out with his friend, Kevin, in the Chris-Craft he had begun to value his separateness. The family was okay, but Kevin and his girlfriend were thrilling. They talked about things together he'd never even heard discussed: especially sex. He caught some of the allusions, but often he didn't get what they really meant. Kevin looked at him once and said: "Joy and I didn't sleep much last night." "Oh," said Westmont. "I hope you sleep better tonight." Joy laughed and said: "I don't." Then they both cracked up and Westmont thought they were probably laughing at him.

When a few days had passed, Kevin asked if Westmont would like to operate the Chris-Craft while he and Joy skied together. Westmont hesitated.

"There's nothing to it, Westy," Kevin said. "Just steer down the lake, avoid hitting sailboats, and if either of us falls the other will let go their rope and all you need to do is circle around, throttle down, and pick us up. But Westy, we never fall. Come on, Buddy, give it a try."

"Would you, Westy," said Joy. And she gave him a little kiss on his cheek.

"Okay, Kevin, I'll try."

Once they were in the water, Kevin and Joy spaced themselves about ten feet apart between what would be the deep left and right waves the wake of the Chris-Craft would make. Westmont could only see their heads bobbing in the water and the tips of their skis pointing up at the sky. He knew that when the rope was taut enough a single motion would bring them both to the surface. He'd seen them do it, one at a time, many times by now. It was strange. If they bent their arms at the elbow trying to pull themselves up, they'd fall right on their faces, the way he himself had done every time he'd tried to get up on skis. "Keep your elbows locked," Kevin had shouted to him, "and let the boat do the work. Don't try to pull yourself up." The rope was suddenly taut and Westmont gunned the engine. Kevin and Joy came up out of the water at once and looked as if they could walk on it in robes of glory if they chose. They were both shouting something. Together they crossed over the left wake, and then

34

back across it and over the right. Slowly they steered themselves back to the calm water directly behind the Chris-Craft and closer and closer together. They were close enough that Kevin could put his arm around Joy. Then they kissed. Westmont was so overcome by this that he kept watching the two of them rather than where he was going. When he turned, a sailboat was on a tack that would bring it in front of the Chris-Craft from the port side. He shut down the throttle and the engine died. Kevin and Joy suddenly sank, both of them laughing and waving their hands above their heads.

"Come and get us," Kevin cried.

But Westmont was stuck, dead in the water. He wasn't sure how to turn the engine on. Kevin and Joy kicked off their skis, and started swimming one-armed toward the boat, trailing the skis behind them with the other arm. With this awkward kind of dog paddle, they finally got to the Chris-Craft, passing the skis up to Westmont and then climbing aboard from the three-step ladder at the stern. When Joy came up, Westy could see her breasts underneath the swimsuit top. She gave him a grin as she climbed aboard, and pulled up the top.

Timothy Westmont remembered that he hadn't bought a hat at the shop. That had been his intention. He'd become distracted by the books and by Deborah Steinbeck. He was annoyed because his dermatologist had warned him sternly not to go out in the sun without protection; he'd had three different pre-cancerous lesions removed from his scalp in the last year. He'd intended to go looking for Patoskey stones today, which had been another favorite pastime during his youthful visits to the lake. These lovely stones were formed during the Devonian period, about 400 million years ago, and they were, or had been, plentiful in and along the small northern lakes and the Lake Michigan shoreline by the town they were named for. Westmont had a small collection at home and thought he'd add to it if he could. But he had forgotten to buy a hat.

Rubbing the top of his balding head, Westmont hurried along the public access path and into the screened porch door of his cottage. Taking off the lid of the carry-out cup, he sipped some of the coffee as he put the books on the table beside his doughnut. He sat down and began thumbing in the books. Some wretched student had defaced all three with a yellow magic marker. In the text of "The Big Two-Hearted River" the following sentence was magically marked: "He had wet his hand before he touched the trout, so he would not disturb the delicate mucus that covered him." In the margin, the reader had written: "Compassionate." Westmont especially disliked the typical wide and looping hand writing of young girls, and this he identified at once, even before he saw this one's name on the inside back cover: Shirley Johnson. Underneath that Shirley had written: "Junior English," and then an address and phone number. That seemed about right, a Junior in high school. Westmont looked for some more markings and comments. "He did not want to rush his sensations any," the author wrote of Nick Adams. And Shirley remarked: "Savoring!" The yellow brick road travelled on: "He sat on the logs, smoking, drying in the sun, the sun warm on his back, the river shallow ahead entering the woods, curving into the woods, shallows, light glittering, big water-smooth rocks, cedars along the bank and white birches…" And Shirley wrote: "Loses emotion." But certainly Shirley was wrong. And certainly wrong again when she wrote: "Leaves his big problems behind. Nick in control." Poor Nick's "big problems" were far too big to be left behind, they were only put aside when he concentrated on landing the trout, Westmont remembered. He turned the page and Nick Adams "worked the trout, plunging, the rod bending alive… holding it then above his head as he led the trout to the net, then lifted." There was a note on a folded sheet of notebook paper between the pages. Westmont opened it. "Can you come round to my house tonight? My parents are going out until about midnight. Junior." This was followed by an address, the same address as the one inside the back jacket. Westmont had guessed wrong. Junior English was a name, not an identification of the high school class in which *In Our Time* had been read. How far out of Hemingway's time were silly Shirley and Junior, and how far out of Shirley and Junior's time was Timothy Westmont. He closed the book but continued to think about fishing.

He was in a boat with his father, trolling in Walloon Lake in 1952. It was an old leaky rowboat with a five horsepower outboard attached. Westmont was using a complicated fishing lure with four sets of nasty hooks and a sinker, which meant that the lure would wiggle and sparkle, attracting fish about eight feet down and maybe bottom-feeders even lower in the weeds. He'd only ever fished much with his father, and he wasn't all that interested in doing it now. He was daydreaming about Kevin and Joy and the Chris-Craft. Kevin had even invited him to play poker with the regulars around the big oak table in the main lodge after dinner. He'd said they'd teach him three-card draw. Westmont had seen this group after dinners in the lodge on his way back to his cabin in the woods. The players were all older than he was, but a couple of them looked closer to his age than Kevin's. It was hard to be sure. He could put people in three categories: Old, like his grandparents; pretty old, like his parents and his teachers; and young, like himself and his cousins. The whole range of ages between his own age and his parents' was always confusing. He knew this was something he needed to work on.

There was a tug at his line.

"Westy," his father said. "You've got a bite."

"I've got more than that," Westmont said. "This is something big."

He had let the line play out a bit as he'd been taught, and then slowly started reeling it in. There was little resistance at first, but a lot of weight. Westmont thought he might just have snagged some heavy weed or a sodden piece of sunken driftwood. But then there was some movement on the water's surface. He saw it was indeed a fish, but not one with a lot of fight left in it. He reeled and reeled and brought it up to the boat. His father dipped in the net and pulled out a large bass. The whole right side of its face was torn by a hook that had entered just behind its eye and then protruded through it. The outer gills had been torn almost off. The sight made Westmont slightly sick. His father took the bass from the net and began to dislodge the hook.

"I didn't really catch it," Westy said. "It was just swimming around and got hooked in the eye by the lure."

"Sure you caught it," his father said. "That's the way these lures work. They attract the fish and once they're close enough the movement of the lure hooks them some place or another."

"But not in the mouth," Westy said. "If you really catch a fish, you hook it in the mouth. Kevin fishes with flies and nothing like this ever happens."

"Forget it," his father said, annoyed. He pulled out the hook and the fish's eye fell to the bottom of the boat and lay there, staring. "I'll put it in the picnic basket and we'll have them cook it for dinner. Let's go back to the Inn."

"But I didn't catch it right," Westy said. I don't want to eat it. All the rest of you can have it if you like."

At dinner, everyone had made a great fuss over the catch. There were twelve of them—three pairs of uncles and aunts, his parents, the cousins, and himself. The Shadow Trails chef had gutted and cleaned the bass for dinner, presenting it at the table with a flourish.

"I weighed it before I cooked it," he said. It's eight pounds. Impressive. More than enough for everyone."

"Not for me," said Westy. "Just pass the potatoes and veg."

Everyone else took a portion of the bass and expressed their pleasure. Westy just sulked, eating a couple of French fries and a few green beans.

Suddenly he was aware that Kevin was standing beside him at the table.

"I'd sure like a taste of that bass," he said. "I saw you reel it in." He had a fork with him and reached over Westy's shoulder to help himself to a piece of the fish. "That's really good," he said. "Cooked just right." As he walked back to the table he was shearing with Joy and her parents, he added: "See you at the poker table."

"You're going to play poker with those big kids after dinner?" his father asked. "You're only twelve years old."

His mother gave his father a stern look. "Kevin's really a nice boy," she said. "He liked the bass. You sure you won't try some?"

"Okay, I'll try some," said Westy.

There was no serious gambling at the poker table; this was penny-ante. But all the players seemed to take it very seriously. They were all boys—or men—though a few girls, including Joy, came now and then to the round table to watch for a while before going back to their conversations around the fireplace or to their books. Westy learned the rules quickly and even won a couple of hands. During the game, Kevin brought up the narrow creek that ran from the lake at the south-east end. Westy had asked him about it earlier. He now explained that it was possible to go up that creek for some distance, but only in a canoe, and only if you were willing to portage in a couple of places. A couple of the other boys had done it, and one of them said, "It can be a lot of fun, but it's swampy and full of insects. Wear lots of repellant and make sure not to get out to portage without sticking an oar in the mud. That place is full of quicksand." Westmont was thinking that he would go up the creek in the Shadow Trails canoe. As if he were reading his thoughts, Kevin suddenly said: "Would you like to go up the creek with me in a couple of days?"

"Don't forget to take a paddle," one of the boys laughed. "And don't shit in the creek. If you did that, what would you be up?" All the others started laughing then and Westmont knew he had failed to catch a joke.

He sat at the porch table in the present wondering why it was that Kevin had paid any attention to him in the past. That particular past was such a long time ago. Even the past of Shirley and Junior was a long time ago. He thumbed in Dr. Cappel's *Hemingway in Michigan*. There were photographs of the lake with very few houses on the shore, photographs of a deserted logging camp. The young friends among the summer people called each other funny names: Buttstein, Pudge Bump, Fartface, Chippawa. For some reason Hemingway's name was Wemege. In the stories, sometimes he used real names for people who appeared as characters. Real people with made up names and made up people with real names. When Dr. Cappel interviewed the locals in the Sixties, many said their parents and uncles and aunts had been bothered by that. They didn't like the mixing up of fiction and fact. That kind of thing still troubles people. There must have been a suicide gene in the Hemingway family: His father, a brother, a sister, a son, and even the granddaughter who made a movie with Woody Allen. He thought her name was Margaux, or was it Mariel? Pretty girl. Hemingway said the Indian girl he first had sex with here was the best fuck he'd ever had. Probably statutory rape, but who would have reported it and who would have cared? He still couldn't print "Go fuck yourself" as late as *For Whom the Bell Tolls* but wrote instead the rather lovely, "Go and obscenity thyself." Necessity: the mother of invention. No intimate personal pronoun left in English. Used to be. Even Norman Mailer was forced to write "Fugg" as an expletive in *The Naked and the Dead*. To thy own self do this or that. That was one lesson Mellors had for Lady Chatterley. Banned book, he'd read it in high school. Dr. Cappel says the Indian girl disappeared from history, which isn't a big surprise. Her parents were some of the last Ottawa bark-peelers. Illiterate all of them. For some reason or other Westmont started thinking about a friend of his, a woman in her seventies still in deep mourning for a husband who had died two or three years before. She told him that her husband's phone message was still playing when she called the old office number. She listened to it every night before she went to sleep: "Hi there, this is Roger Lincoln in the math department. Please leave a message and I'll call you back." Westmont wondered what his friend would do with her grief when someone finally got around to erasing the message. Westmont didn't use what his mother called cusswords himself. His father did though, and his mother always said when he did that it showed he had a small vocabulary. Even at Shadow Trails Inn at that big family table. He'd spill something on his shirt and more or less automatically mumble, "God damn the goddam goddam damn." Ezra Pound, "Winter is icummen in. Lhude, sing goddamn." Not "sing cuckoo." The back garden here was full of birds, especially cardinals and finches. Territorial, birds. Is that what they were singing about, or was it sex? Were they monogamous? They came back in pairs, looking just like last year's lot. Suppose you could only tell if you banded a leg. They all look alike, year after year, millennium after millennium. If he phoned the number on the inside cover of *In Our Time*, would someone answer saying, "Junior English residence"? People with names like Junior all looked alike. Had motorcycles rather than cars. What about people called Timothy? Did they all look alike? People called Westy, Westmont, Buddy? Kevin had probably liked him because Kevin was likable himself. Nice to everyone. Even though he looked like a god. The young Paul Newman was like that, or so they said. But not Hemingway, who could be very nasty and mean. Walked one summer all the way from Oak Park to Horton Bay. About three hundred miles. Wemedge. His Ottawa lover, his Chicago girlfriend Buttstein. The whole generation was anti-Semitic. Buttstein retaliated with Hemingstein. His books also full of the N word; what would a modern editor do with the Nigger boxer in *The Sun Also Rises*? Some solution, certainly. White folks now hardly dare invent a black character. Jews write about Jews. His cruel portrait of Robert Cohen, Jew from Princeton, boxer. Latinos will doubtless inherit the earth. Or Chinese. His wife was somewhere in England, probably back in Suffolk. Cold and rainy county, he'd been told. He'd never been there himself, just in London once or twice. Not much of a traveller. In his nerdish way he sometimes liked to say during political discussions with friends that he favored the restoration of the British Empire. Didn't really mean that, but it tended to end those discussions since people thought he was serious and were embarrassed for him. Muhqua Nebis, Bear Lake, Walloon now but no Walloons around.

Westmont woke from his reverie because Harvey Schach was tapping lightly on the screen door with a bottle of wine under his arm and two glasses in his hand. "Like to share a bottle of Chablis?" he said. "It's nice and cold."

Westmont let him in and Schach sat down at the table. He poured the wine into the glasses and offered a toast: "To the Lake!"

"To the Lake!" Westmont echoed, and had a sip of the Chablis. "How's work going on your boats?"

"The work always goes just fine, but there are very few sales. The lake used to be full of Seventeens."

"I see a two or three just looking off this porch."

"Sold those years ago. The kids like jet skis and my generation is far too old to sail. That leaves your generation. How about buying a Seventeen? The very one you've been admiring in the front drive. I'll even repaint it if you don't like the color. Throw in the trailer for free."

"How much?" Westmont asked.

"Forty-five thousand. Forty-three if you pour me another glass of wine."

"I can't afford the boat, but I'm glad to pour the Chablis."

"Have you been on the lake at all?"

"Not yet, but I thought I'd see if I could paddle the canoe around the left fork there and look for a creek I knew about when we stayed at Shadow Trails."

"I know that creek," said Harvey. "It's very narrow and even the lake at that point is pretty much silted up. Memory lane, is it?"

"What do you mean?"

"Something happen there that you want to revisit?"

"It's more like something that didn't happen."

"People your age are nostalgic. People my age have got beyond nostalgia. Sometimes I see a whole pontoon boat full of men your age getting drunk and making a great fuss about some fishing they did up here when they were young. The more they drink the louder they talk. You can hear them halfway across the lake. It really cracks me up. I could tell them where all the fish are now when I see them in the village, but I don't breathe a word. I hope you're not one of those Hemingway nuts?" He pointed at the books on the table.

"Haven't read him for years. The woman in the general store convinced me I should borrow a couple of books."

"Good Lord," Harvey said. "You've also got Doctor Constance Cappel. She drove us all nuts when she was nosing around in the sixties. She picked my brain for a bit, but I didn't know very much. She really bothered the folks in Horton Bay, especially the owners of the store and post office. But she met her match when she stumbled into the Petoskey Hemingway Club. They're a bunch of drunks who meet at the City Grill, which still has the very long bar where the master used to drink with his buddies when he was young. Nice place, really. The tin roof is also unchanged. Big fireplace in the winter. Anyway, the PHC led her on so much she didn't know what to believe and what not to. They even got her doing the E.H. divination game."

"What's that?"

"Oh, you know. Open a book and put your finger down on a passage. It will predict your future. People do it with the Bible or the Koran. But only that lot ever did it with the Nick Adams stories. You want to try? Open the book—not the Cappel thing, *In Our Time*."

He opened the book and, without looking, put his finger down: *A short time after he contracted gonorrhea*. "That doesn't sound very good," he said. "These guys really did this? In earnest, as it were?"

"Very funny. Try again."

"Want to hear the annotation?"

"What do you mean?"

"I'm an anal archivist and I always notice these things. Even collect them. At the bottom of the page our annotator writes: *This is really gross.*

"Some scholar wrote that?"

"No, the previous owner, a high-school girl called Shirley Johnson who wrote in the book before it ended up in the General Store's lending library. Her boyfriend was Junior English. She wrote his name and address in the book."

"She married him," Harvey said. "I knew both of them. It's a tight knit community up here. But try the divination again."

Westmont opened the book, put down his finger toward the end of it. *"He was settled. Nothing could touch him. It was a good place to camp. He was there, in the good place. He was in his home where he had made it."*

"Ah ha!" said Schach. "You see, maybe there's something to it. I feel that myself now and then about this place. I used to come up here just in the summers, but it's the only place I've ever been happy. I signed my business in Cleveland over to my nephew and started staying up here through the winters. Love it. There are very few of us around the lake itself in heavy weather, though skiers go to Boyne Mountain if there's the right kind of snow. Chuck Moll ran the Mountain and Shadow Trails both. I'm pretty sure he would have been in charge when you were there. Name ring a bell?"

"It does. He was very nice to Kevin McBride, a kid who was the champion water-skier and fisherman when I was there. But he was an austere kind of man and formal with the rest of us to the point of seeming cold. But Kevin McBride brought something out in him."

"Oh well," said Schach, "we all admired Kevin McBride."

"You knew him?"

"Everybody knew him. Spirit of the place, you know, for a few years. You were lucky to have met him. He also had the world's most lovely girlfriend, Joy Morgan, who spent her summers here with her family. Kevin was year-round, like I am now. They were just teenagers then, but very grown up in terms of the way they dealt with each other and people in general. Kevin was one of the most generous kids I've ever known."

"He was certainly generous to me," said Westmont. "But there was also a time when I thought he'd let me down. I was allowed in on all the older boys' sports and games; Kevin even let me drive his Chris-Craft. He let me play poker with his friends. It seemed perfectly natural to me since he seemed so entirely easy about it all. But my father was worried about it, I think, maybe suspected he was homosexual."

"Kevin?" Harvey exclaimed. "Not a chance. That kid was just magnanimous; I saw it again and again. He probably thought you were lonely."

"I *was* lonely. And also a loner. I guess I still am."

"You see? But what did he do to let you down?"

"Oh, he didn't. I just thought so briefly."

"What happened?" Harvey filled my glass with Chablis.

"It's a hard story to tell," said Westmont. "At first I was utterly confused by what I was seeing and then totally broken up by it."

"You don't have to tell me," Harvey said. "We can talk about something else."

"It's okay. It was a long time ago. I've mentioned the proposed canoe trip up the creek, the one I may actually try to make in a day or so. Anyway, we had set a time for it and I was waiting for Kevin in the canoe. He was late and pretty soon he was very late. I got up on the dock and paced back and forth. The lake was absolutely still, not a ripple. No boats were out. I forgot to mention it was very early in the morning. We had decided to go before most people were up. I thought maybe Kevin had overslept. Then I had the thought that maybe he'd decided he had something more important to do than go early-morning canoeing with a kid, and I got a little angry. I waited for him for a full hour. The first couple of swimmers came down from the lodge and greeted me. Then I saw one of my uncles with his fishing pole. A motorboat passed by making a wake, and the canoe bounced against the broken wood of the dock. I walked up to the lodge and could see my parents having breakfast through the window. I decided to go back to bed.

"Our cabin was the second farthest from the lodge, so it was a bit of a walk. I was still feeling very let down. When I got to the cabin I could hear voices coming from the one next door, a cabin pretty isolated in the woods. You think at this point you know what's coming in this story, but you don't."

"I think I probably do," said Harvey Schach. He poured both of them another glass of Chablis, emptying the bottle. "But go ahead."

"No, you don't. Because it was the sound of terrible weeping. When I got up to the window and peeked over, I saw Kevin lying on the bed and Joy kind of holding her head as if it hurt and walking around the room. Then she sat down in a chair and Kevin got up and *he* walked around. 'I'm so scared,' he said. 'I'm so damn scared.' Joy sat there with her head still in her hands. Then Kevin knelt down before her and put his head in her lap, and she took her hands off her own head and put them on his. At this point I remembered older kids telling me about things a man

43

could do with his tongue in a woman's crotch, and then Joy really started weeping—louder and louder—and I thought Kevin was doing that thing, but he kept saying he was so scared, and Joy said she was so scared too, and it was just horrible, horrible, and I didn't know what to do. I was sure all this was about sex, and half realized I'd been thinking about sex between the two of them from the time I'd met them. Kevin then actually said to her, 'And I've left that Westmont kid waiting for me. Damn it all to hell. You'd think I could be a man about this and not fall all apart.' And Joy said, 'Why shouldn't you fall all apart? Forget about the kid and think about us. What are we going to do?' And Kevin laughed then, in a kind of crazy way, and said: 'Well I know what I'm going to do. What are you going to do?' And Joy said, 'I think I'm going to fall all apart.' Kevin said, 'We can't both fall apart.' By this time I felt pretty much like I was going to fall all apart myself, and I jumped up and pounded at the window. I said, 'Hey Kevin, you forgot about the canoe,' not because that made any sense at that point, even to me, but because it was the only thing I could think to say. They both more of less jumped out of their skins with surprise, and there I was at the window, grinning like an idiot. They both tried to stop crying. Kevin stood up, wiping his eyes and looking really strange. He bent over to Joy and I could just barely hear him saying, 'Can you talk to him? Tell him to ask... to explain.' But I couldn't make out the name. Joy walked to the cabin door, wiping her own eyes. She looked round the corner, where I was still standing in front of the window. 'Come here, Timothy,' she said. I didn't know why she was calling me Timothy, since neither of them had done that at all. I was always Westy. Joy was looking really angry when she waved me toward the door, and I had the sense that I'd done something terribly wrong. 'Look, Timothy, she said. This is a really difficult time for us. Please don't ask Kevin what it's all about. And don't ask me. Go ask Chuck Moll. Now go away, please go away.'"

"Being sent to Chuck Moll was kind of like being sent to the school Principal. He owned the place, after all, and, as I said, he always had seemed a kind of tough and forbidding presence, though he also clearly had this special fondness for Kevin. He dealt mostly with adults, and mainly with their money. But I was so confused that I went straight to the lodge and did what Joy had asked. Chuck Moll had an office just to the side of the common room, the one with the fireplace where the boys played poker and the girls gossiped and read, where he kept his accounts, made phone calls, and interviewed workmen. The door was open and he was behind his desk. I blundered in breathlessly and asked if we could talk. 'Talk?' he said. 'Yes,' I said. 'About Kevin and Joy.' He looked at me with what I could now only call utter contempt: 'Why do you want to talk to me about Kevin and Joy?' 'Because Joy asked me to,' I said. 'They're both very upset?' 'How do you know they're upset?' he asked. 'I saw them crying in the cabin on the hill.' Chuck Moll gave me another contemptuous look: 'You've been looking in on them?' 'It was about the canoe,' I said, 'and the trip up the creek. Kevin didn't show up.' Moll's expression became a little more friendly: 'You're with the Westmont party, aren't you?' 'We're not really having a party,' I said, 'but that's my family. We all eat together, but we're different…', and I didn't know or couldn't say what different things we were. Chuck Moll said: 'I suppose you mean you're different branches of the same family.' I said that was it, though I wasn't sure it was."

At this point Westmont was half drunk and half dazed by the pressure of the past. But why this particular past? He'd not thought about Kevin and Joy for many years. And he certainly hadn't come to Walloon Lake to think about them now. He had come to up north to stop thinking about anything for a while, especially his mother and his wife. Perhaps it had been a bad choice. He might have gone to Carmel, or Big Sur. Those places would have brought the Sixties back, not the Fifties. A decade meant such a lot then, from being a kid to being married with a job. Harvey Schach saw that Westmont was beginning to lose it. He still figured that Harvey thought his story was all about sex, when you got down to it. Who was it said that everything is about sex except sex? Or was it that everything's about death except death? Or maybe everything's about both, and one shouldn't dwell on it?

"Most of us knew that Kevin was dying," he said. "But it must have come as a shock to you, especially if you got the news from Chuck Moll."

"That's putting it mildly," Westmont said.

"How did he tell you?"

"Brutally," I said. "He told me that Kevin had leukemia and wouldn't live through the winter. I had to ask him what leukemia was, and he simply said 'an almost always fatal blood cancer. He's already had all the treatments he's going to get. Joy's going to marry him, even though she knows he's going to die and they're both under age. Leave them alone. They're both very nice people, but they need to be left alone. Don't keep tagging along.'"

"I couldn't think of anything to say. He's"—I stopped for a moment—"beautiful and strong. You're telling me he's sick?" He shrugged: "He'll be dead by New Year, 1953. There's nothing more the doctors can do."

At this point Harvey Schack interrupted Westmont again. "You can't imagine how many versions of this story I've heard. Kevin had so many friends. Not a single one of them talked to him about his illness. Joy had to bear it all. By the time he actually died, all the summer people had left the lake, even Joy and her clan. Of course their families wouldn't let them marry. In the end, Kevin was so sick he didn't care one way or another. There's so much more the doctors can do for that condition today."

"But I've not finished the story," Westmont said.

"But we have finished the wine."

Harvey Schach stood up to leave, and Westmont let it go at that. He thought a bit about stories, and how they are never finished. That whole Nick Adams chronicle was mainly a broken mirror, various shards reflecting this thing and that. He had a sense that he could learn much more if he returned to the village shop and got to know Deborah Steinbeck. But he decided not to. For a moment he indulged a fantasy: That Joy had married Kevin after all. That somehow he'd survived his illness. Funny, that. Chuck Moll would have said it couldn't have happened, and Harvey Schach would have agreed. But if he wrote fiction, Westmont could make it happen in some magical way. But he was just a collector of valuable books and manuscripts, a collector of other people's stories.

The last time he'd seen Kevin had been at the dock, two days following his terrible eavesdropping at the cottage adjacent to his own. Kevin seemed just the same. He was in the Chris-Craft and about to go out alone for a ride in the unusually rough lake.

"Hey, Westy," he said. "How'd you like to have this boat? I won't be needing it next summer. Like to have it? Want to have a Chris-Craft of your own?"

"Are you serious?" Westmont asked.

"Of course not," Kevin said. "But want to go for a ride?"

"Oh, no thanks. I told my dad I'd go out with him looking for Petoskey stones."

Westmont was a bit surprised that such a lot had happened in one day. But how much was that? Only a walk to the shop and two conversations. The next week passed pleasantly enough, and he even managed to paddle the canoe all the way past Shadow Trails to the creek. He didn't go down it, but he had a good look. It was very swampy on both sides, and the water was black. He suddenly imagined himself pulling his boat by a rope tied around his chest out into the lake once it had become stuck in the mud, like Humphrey Bogart did, covered with leeches, in *The African Queen*. He remembered Bogey shivering with horror as Katherine

Hepburn pulled the blood-sucking creatures off his back and thighs. "I hate leeches!" Bogey had said. Bogey and Westy, both with a story to tell. Westmont hadn't quite managed to tell his own correctly to Harvey Schach, and maybe even told entirely the wrong story. That would have been just like him. He should have asked Harvey to tell a story instead. Westmont bet he had some good ones. If he could have afforded a Seventeen he'd have thought about staying up here for good and learning to sail.

Once he got home Westmont looked up some old articles from the Petoskey newspaper on his archive computer. Surprisingly, a lot had been saved from the old microfilms and transferred over to digital records. Kevin had died right on schedule, shortly after New Year 1953, and his ashes had been scattered in the lake. Joy had married someone called Jeremy Steinbeck, but he had left her a few years after he bought the Walloon Lake general store from Harvey Schach, of Cleveland. The store was part of the divorce settlement. She had run the place herself for more than thirty years.

Westmont and the Different Kinds of Music

2

Westmont's paternal grandfather really only liked marches, though sometimes he made an exception for pieces like Tchaikovsky's *Overture of 1812*. He had fought in the Spanish-American War and his own father had fought in the Civil War where he was wounded at the battle of Shiloh. That's why Westmont's grandfather was given "Shiloh" for a middle name. In Westmont's early youth, one public park in Columbus still had a bandstand in which a military band played public concerts on Saturday mornings. It was mostly the music of John Phillip Sousa. When Westmont went to these concerts with his grandfather he always asked if he could take along one of the swords stashed in a large walk-in closet in the old family home that also contained Grandfather's and Great-Grandfather's Civil War and Spanish-American War dress uniforms, all of them with gleaming gold epaulettes. Westy would hold the sword on his lap as if it were a precious relic from the past, which, after all, it was. Only when the band ended its performance with a march containing an almost maniacal piccolo solo would he step from his seat, unsheathe the sword, and, as he thought, conduct the band himself from the grass sward with a baton nearly as long as he was tall. Many in the audience would applaud this embarrassing stunt. Once, the actual conductor even turned and bowed to him.

Westmont and the Bagpipe Music

aeiooooumph—

or something like that, and Westmont woke up with a start. It was late on Halloween night, long after the kids had been around for trick-or-treat, but Westmont's first thought was that the noise must be connected to some kind of Halloween-related prank. *Aeiooomph blaugghaiiiiium.* When he looked at the clock beside his bed he saw that it was very late indeed—or very early if you like—just past 3:00 a.m. The noise continued, but was it exactly a noise? He got up to look out the window and was embarrassed to find Mrs. Hathscant in her nightdress staring out of her own lighted window into the street between their houses, and then looking up at him and giving a little wave. He sat back down on his bed. *Rummmmphaweddioooph.* Not noise exactly, but a kind of music. And then he had it: pipes. A bagpipe player at three o'clock a.m. What the hell?

He looked out the window again. A few more lights had come on in houses along the street. A man he didn't know was out on his front porch, looking up and down the sidewalk. Mrs. Hathscant had now turned on her living room light and could be seen standing near a large chair beside her fireplace. The piping continued. It is indeed a resonant instrument, he thought, especially in the dead quiet of the predawn hours when even the burglars who sometimes broke into cars parked along the curb—there were few garages in this part of town—had called it a night and gone home to bed. He put on his bathrobe and came downstairs. Wide awake now, he poured himself a glass of wine. The piper must be somewhere walking back and forth, because the sound grew a little louder and then a little softer; there was almost a Doppler effect.

It is a mournful music, he thought. Maybe something like the beginning of an Indian raga, before the drumming begins and the tempo increases. But what did he know about ragas? What did he know, for that matter, about pipes?

He knew a little about Janet Hathscant. As a divorcé himself, he'd looked once or twice with interest at the widow across the street. They were both in their early fifties, both fairly fit and good looking. From time to time there seemed to be some chemistry between them. Once at a neighborhood Christmas party they had been a little drunk and exchanged kisses like teenagers on the basement landing as they left by a side door to return to their respective homes. The next day, when they met in the street scraping the windshields of their cars following a heavy frost, they had both blushed for a moment, though neither had made reference to the incident the night before. In fact, Westmont continued to call her Mrs. Hathscant out of respect for her late husband. Once she ventured to call him by his dreaded nickname—Westy—because she had heard an old friend of his doing so. But she had only done that once. He took his glass of wine to the front window and looked again into the street. A few people had gathered there. They stood together under a streetlight and seemed to be talking together quietly. After a moment, Mrs. Hathscant opened her front door and joined them. She had put on a raincoat and a hat. It was impossible to tell if she still wore her nightdress underneath or had changed into something else. He thought he might go out.

He thought he could better sense the direction of the piping from his front porch, so he put on a pair of shoes, opened the door, and sat down on his new wicker swing. He swung. *Swing, swang, swung* he incanted to himself. *Sing, sang, sung.* A gray cat crept out of the long grass at the edge of his modest property. *Runummmphaweddiooophwoo.* It was certainly louder now, and he could tell that the piper had turned about-face and was headed back in the direction of the neighbors by the street lamp. He guessed that the music came from beyond the tall hedge on the street one block west that ran beside the city park. It was a nice enough park, he thought. The city had been on an economic downturn ever since the collapse of the big auto parts company in the 1970s, but they kept up their parks. In good weather he crossed it on his walk up to the college. But he knew that it was no longer safe at night; there were drug deals and other nefarious activities going on down there once it got dark. Still, he also knew that young couples risked being robbed or mugged by going to the park at night for sex. Once he had seen between the ears of a plastic zebra playground toy—molded and welded on a steel spring so that giggling children could bounce on it—a nasty used condom.

Westmont was chief archivist at the college. As he had been at his post for a good number of years, he was privy to some of the institution's darker secrets. People died and left their papers to the archive and mostly no one bothered to read them except for Westmont. By that time, of course, it was too late for anyone to care about the secrets any more. Colleagues valued his tact and reticence. He very rarely let on what he knew.

Damn, he thought. It's got to be Mike McElroy.

Years ago McElroy had asked him if he could deposit what he thought might someday prove to be a valuable correspondence in the archive. It turned out to be a cache of letters between a Scottish poet and McElroy's mother—not another McElroy, but a Mc or Mac something else—on the subject of Piobaireachd, the classical form of Highland piping. It was coming back to him. This poet had written a long poem in Gaelic on the *Ceol Mor* Laments and McElroy's mother had engaged him in some questions asked on behalf of the Piobairechd Society of which she was a member. There were also some letters that seemed to be personal, and, without more than glancing at them, Westmont put those under a twenty-year seal. McElroy had never mentioned that he played the pipes himself, but he lived just a block away over that hedge and that's where the piping was coming from. Who else? The other thing about McElroy was that he ought really to have been called Malkiel. That was his father's name when he married the red-haired Scottish girl at the outset of World War II. Because he was Jewish and had no idea what the outcome of the war would be, they decided it would be safest to make McElroy the family name. But Mike had hardly known his father. Soon after the end of the war Malkiel had left for Palestine, which, during the period of the British Mandate, was a place Mike's mother refused to go. That, Westmont suspected, was a very short version of a long and complicated story, but it was enough at the time for him to understand something of the background of Mrs. McElroy's correspondence with the Scottish poet.

As he reflected on this sudden memory, a car drove slowly down the street with red lights flashing. Someone had called the police.

The only other thing that Westmont knew about McElroy—strangely it still ruffled his feathers—was that he had in a way been responsible for that Christmas party kiss between himself and Mrs. Hathscant. McElroy had been flirting with her himself off and on through the party. After a good deal of drinking, they had been seen with arms around each other in a casually friendly way. This had made Westmont suddenly and quite irrationally jealous—McElroy was a good fifteen years older than he was, and might even be referred to as elderly. In spite of his heavy steel-gray hair and his thin waist, he was just this side of being *old*. It was soon after making these observations that Westmont and Mrs. Hathscant exited by the basement-landing door and exchanged their kiss. He felt quite ridiculous thinking about it now. As the police car stopped beside the group of neighbors under the streetlight, he walked down his front porch steps and headed in their direction. A woman he didn't recognize was chasing a small human skeleton down the sidewalk. When he stopped and stared, she said her son had gone to bed in his costume and, with all the commotion, had awakened and run out the door to see what it was all about. "It's just Mike McElroy," said Westmont, feeling quite confident now that he was right.

Given that confidence, he had the sense that he ought, as it were, to take charge. He put his empty wine glass on the porch railing and headed toward the group under the streetlight where the police car had now pulled up and stopped. Along with Mrs. Hathscant, the group included three men he'd seen around the neighborhood but didn't know by name and the little skeleton with his mother. As Westmont walked up to them the policeman got out of his car.

"Do you know the individual who's making all the noise," he asked. "We've had a lot of calls. I could drive over there and just shut him up, but maybe it would be better if a neighbor asked him politely."

"The *person* who's playing the *music* is probably Michael McElroy," said Westmont, surprised that he'd let himself sound huffy about the officer's "individual" and "noise." Why was everyone an "individual" these days? And none of these individuals had problems any longer either; they all had "issues."

"The basic issue," said the officer, "is that people want to sleep. What kind of music is it anyway? "

"Piobaireachd," said Westmont.

"What?"

"I think it's bagpipe music. I didn't know that Michael McElroy could play the pipes, but he once let me see a very technical correspondence between his mother and a Scottish poet on the subject."

"His mother and a Scottish poet."

"Yes. He was given his mother's name at birth, or so he told me, because his father was Jewish during the war against Hitler and they were afraid there might be an invasion."

"Are you talking about the Scottish poet?"

"No, about Mike McElroy. His mother belonged to the Edinburgh Piobaireachd Society and we were given some of her papers, including the correspondence with the poet on classical Scottish piping."

"You were given some of her papers?"

"The college archive was."

"About playing the bagpipes?"

"Yes."

"And this is what makes you think that Mr. McElroy is playing the bagpipes now and keeping everyone awake?"

"Now that I think of it, he told me when depositing the papers that I should probably use the hyphenated name Malkiel-McElroy, as he wanted it in the record that his father had once been part of the family."

"Part of the family?"

"Yes. I suppose there was a time during the war when they thought that might be a solution regarding the name—to hyphenate it, I mean. But they decided on McElroy."

"They decided on McElroy?"

"Yes. But I don't really know Michael very well. He took early retirement from his department a few years ago in order to pursue various hobbies."

"Like playing the bagpipes at three o'clock in the morning?"

Westmont by now understood that he must be sounding like an idiot. Everyone was grinning at him, even Mrs. Hathscant. The little skeleton said very audibly to his mother, "What's the bagpipes?" Westmont said, "Why don't we just walk over to Michael's place and ask him to call it a night?"

And so they all trailed along: Westmont leading the way, the policeman walking beside him, and the five others following. During this whole time there had been no let up in the piping. If anything it seemed louder now that everybody agreed on what it was they heard and that it was probably Michael McElroy who was responsible. Everybody seemed to be in a very jolly mood. The three men that Westmont didn't know by name introduced themselves as Steve Fredman, William O'Rourke, and John Wilkinson. His friends Jay Walton and Ernest Webber were there as well. The mother introduced the little skeleton as Ned and said her own name was Marjorie Kinsey. Mrs. Hathscant gave him a little pat on the shoulder and said, "It's a very late and very extraordinary night." Then they turned the corner beyond the high hedge and saw Michael McElroy striding down the sidewalk with his bagpipes. When he got to the cross street, he turned smartly on the ball of his left foot and headed directly towards them.

Rummmmphaweddiooph. Westmont heard some repetitions in the melody, if that was what it should be called, and wondered for an instant if this music were written or improvised. McElroy kept on playing, kept on striding towards them. The little skeleton got behind his mother. Walton, O'Rourke, and Webber took a step back. Only Westmont and Mrs. Hathscant stood their ground. On came McElroy. *Rummmphaweddiooph.* And then he suddenly stopped. He let the mouthpiece fall from his lips and the remaining air in the bag made a sound like a weeping walrus— *Oooooooouuuuuuuuummmmmmffffff.* The music stopped. Westmont took a step forward.

"Michael?"

"Who are all these people?" he said.

"Neighbors," Westmont said.

"Mr. McElroy," said the policemen, "You're keeping folks awake."

"I suppose I am."

"Are you all right, Michael?" Westmont asked.

"As a matter of fact, I'm not."

"What's the trouble, Mike?"

"Grief. Grief is the trouble."

"Is there something we can do to help?"

"Do?"

"Do to help? Anything we can do?"

And the policeman said: "Why don't you two friends go inside and the rest of us will just go back where we came from. You've been violating a city noise ordinance and I want you to stop it now. You're not sick or anything?"

"Sick or anything," echoed McElroy.

"I don't think he'll play any more tonight," Westmont said to the officer.

"That's good, that's good." And to McElroy: "You just go on in your house with your friend. And no more music tonight."

"Music," said McElroy. "And he's not really my friend. Only an acquaintance."

"Then you go just go on in with your acquaintance here."

"Acquaintance here."

"Yes, go on in with your acquaintance."

It had become clear that Michael had been drinking a lot. The neighbors nodded a quick good-night and turned to leave. The policeman shook hands with Westmont: "Thanks for your help," he said. Walton, O'Rourke, and Webber didn't look back as they walked away. The little skeleton did. His mother took his hand and pulled him along. Mrs. Hathscant stayed behind. McElroy took both her shoulders in his hands.

"Oh, Janet. I'm a miserable piece of work. I think I've been playing a Salute rather than a Lament, but it's been so many years that I've avoided this machine. I was trying to lament the death of a highland laird."

"Well, it was really pretty, Mike," said Mrs. Hathscant.

"Do you think?"

"Yes, it was really beautiful."

"Michael, would you like to go in?" asked Westmont. "We can all sit and talk for a bit. Maybe that would be the thing to do."

So in they went to Michael McElroy's house. He carried the dead pipes under his arm that looked like a couple of deflated inner tubes.

They still let out a fetid breath now and then until he had stowed them behind a sofa in his living room. "Drinks all around?" he asked with ironic enthusiasm.

"Maybe a coffee," said Mrs. Hathscant.

"A coffee would be good," said Mr. Westmont.

When coffee had been served they began to talk. McElroy told them that he'd had a phone call in the middle of the night from someone identifying himself as his uncle. He was unaware that he even had an uncle. The call was from Tel Aviv and the news was that his father had died at the age of 96 in an Israeli nursing home. He felt immediate and overwhelming grief for this man he had never really known and who had never bothered to get in touch with him either in Scotland or America once he had arrived in Palestine shortly before the proclamation of the state of Israel.

"How did the uncle know how to reach you?" asked Westmont.

"No idea."

"And you thought you'd play your Kaddish on the pipes?"

"First I drank a good deal of good Scotch whisky. I haven't played a Pibroch for a decade or so, though now and then I've done military stuff as a kind of comical presentation for the marching band. I've totally lost the knack, as I'm sure you heard, but for a while my mother sent me to a piping school at the Piobaireachd Academy. I think her revenge against my father's abrupt departure was to make me the only Jewish piper since the emergence of Patrick Mor MacCrimmon and the origin of the tradition. Have you ever been to Skye, home of the MacLeods of Dunvegan? I was once forced to participate in a piping competition there. Humiliating. People actually greeted each other by saying things like *Cha till, cha till, cha till mi tuille. Return, return, return... though MacLeod should return, not alive shall MacCrimmon.* I can't remember one tune from the next any more. I think I may have been playing a greeting for Charles the Second out there. My poor father. My poor mother, too. I don't suppose you get it."

"My mother was a Kirkpatrick," said Westmont.

"Ah."

"But the family was Scotch-Irish. They all came from Belfast."

"And banged on an Orangeman's great drum?"

"I don't think so."

Mrs. Hathscant had by now curled up on a sofa with her legs underneath her. She kept giving Westmont little winks as if she thought the story was all made up. But she also cast a glance now and then at McElroy that Westmont at first couldn't read. Then he had the sudden thought that she might like to see Michael wearing a kilt. He thought about those papers lying in a dark drawer in his archive. The correspondence with the Scottish poet. He assumed Michael had never married, but of course he'd never asked.

"Did you ever marry, Mike?"

"I had lots of girlfriends for a while."

"But never a wife? Sorry, it's really none of my business."

"No one could figure why I was into Biblical Hermeneutics and Midrash."

"You mean this put off the marriageable girls?"

"It was not the coolest field in the Swinging Edinburgh of the 1960s."

"It sounds cool enough to me," put in Mrs. Hathscant.

"Also, it was very hard to find a job. It's a highly specialized field and I couldn't find a position anywhere in Britain. That's why I came here in 1969. The theology department was hiring."

"You never thought about Israel?"

"Of course I thought about Israel. All the time. But everybody does Biblical hermeneutics in Israel and anyway I'd have had to see my spaced-out Zionist father."

"You'd have looked him up?"

"Of course I'd have looked him up."

"Even though he'd left you in the hands of Scottish pipers?"

"He was out building settlements somewhere."

It was clear to Westmont that McElroy had calmed down and was growing sober. He began to think of a way that he and Mrs. Hathscant could say goodnight and leave. He came back to the main question of the night, the father's death. But before he could express final condolences and say goodbye, McElroy spoke up again.

"I suppose you're Catholic, like most of our colleagues."

"No, no. Kirkpatrick, remember? I'm a lapsed Presbyterian."

"A collapsed Presbyterian."

"I guess I'm really nothing anymore."

"Really nothing."

"No."

"Your father was Presbyterian too?"

"My father."

"Mr. Westmont, I presume."

"Lutheran, in fact, to begin with. He became a Presbyterian."

"But he wasn't Scotch-Irish."

Mrs. Hathscant said brightly: "We're still a fine old melting pot in this country, luckily enough. My name was originally Polish, but no one could spell it so I was relieved on that score when I became Mrs. Hathscant."

"I'm sorry for all that noise. It's not the kind of thing I usually do."

"I hope not, " said Westmont, laughing. "We'd never be able to sleep if you usually did it."

"Don't worry, I won't."

"But just this once you thought you had to play the pipes for your father."

"Because he had died."

"Of course. And maybe for your mother too. And the Scottish poet."

"Maybe so. I won't do it again."

"No."

"I never asked you if your mother's still living in Edinburgh," Westmont said.

"She's not living at all. She died some time ago."

"I'm sorry."

"Well," said Mrs. Hathscant, "we should probably be off so everyone can go to bed."

The three of them stood up. Westmont realized for the first time since he had left his house that he was still wearing his bathrobe. It was a heavy winter robe, with a bit of insulation on the inside, so it looked rather like a coat tied with a sash. Still, it didn't look right with the walking shoes he had put on. With sandals or maybe sneakers it would have been all right. His carpet slippers would have done just fine on the sidewalk, but they were new and he hadn't wanted to scuff them.

"Your wife," said McElroy. "Did I ever meet her up at school?"

"I doubt it," Westmont said.

"She was called?"

"Mrs. Westmont," said Westmont.

"Of course."

"And your father?"

"My father."

"He was called?"

"He was called Isaac Malkiel,"said McElroy.

"Well," said Mrs. Hathscant, "that was a beautiful piedbrack you played for him."

"Thank you," said McElroy. "And thanks for stopping by."

Mr. Westmont and Mrs. Hathscant said goodbye, Westmont shaking hands and Mrs. Hathscant giving him a little kiss on the cheek. McElroy shut the door behind them. They began walking slowly to their homes. Lights were now off in all the houses on their block and the fine Halloween mist of an hour before had begun to lift. The moon now shone clearly in a clear sky. When they reached the streetlight where their late night out had begun, Mrs. Hathscant said:

"Do you like Blake?"

"Blake?"

"The poet, you know. *Piping down the valleys wild, piping songs of pleasant glee.* We had to memorize it in school."

"I think that's a different kind of piping entirely," said Westmont.

"Oh, I know. It's just the association of the word. That brought it to mind."

"What do you make of our friend?" he asked.

"Well, I have a kind of confession," she said. "We were once piping pals."

"You were what?"

"Yes. And I knew it was Michael out there from the start. About ten years ago we got acquainted at a folk dancing club in town—polkas and the horah and all that—and he invited me around to hear his pipes as if it were to see his etchings, sort of. My uncle Mickiewicz was a piper too, so I was not entirely unacquainted with the instrument. We played together for a bit. It sounded awful. *Hoosier Piedbracks*, we called our yowling duets."

"Your uncle was a Polish bagpipe player?"

Before she could say *yes* she started saying *no*. Westmont had put his arms around her waist and pulled her to him. He could tell at once that she had nothing on beneath her raincoat but a nightdress. After the muffled protest, she kissed him fully on the mouth, and there was a little flicking of her tongue. They kissed until they both needed to breathe, and then they stood apart and stared at each other, neither of them knowing what to do next.

"So sad about McElroy's father," he said, sounding wholly unsympathetic.

"Yes, Michael's poor father," she said sympathetically.

"Janet?" he asked with some hesitation.

"Westy?" she said.

"Miss Mickiewicz," he said

"Mr. Westmont," she said.

"Mrs. Hathscant," he replied.

Westmont and the Different Kinds of Music

3

The music teacher, Miss Albert, liked Stephen Foster songs, and Westmont's class was asked to sing some of them every Tuesday and Thursday in music class. Many of them were about Negro slaves. Westmont found it all rather troubling; especially as his one good friend who wasn't Jewish was black. Westmont especially hated singing "Old Black Joe." His friend was called Joseph Black. True, no one ever called him Joe; he was always Joseph. Also, he didn't seem to mind the song himself. Along with everyone else, he belted it out with enthusiasm:

> Gone are the days when my heart was young and gay,
> Gone are my friends from the cotton fields away,
> Gone from the earth to a better land I know,
> I hear those darkies' voices calling "Old Black Joe."

Joseph grew up to be an honors student at an eastern university and, eventually, a successful lawyer. When he decided to run for Congress, he started calling himself "Joe." Those were the days of "Jimmy" Carter and, a little later, "Bill" Clinton. Now, if you're famous enough, you don't need a surname at all: Oprah, Madonna, Prince. Granted, Bill or Jimmy or Joe wouldn't make the list of always already sufficient first names. But Westmont always called his old friend Joseph, even when he'd been elected to three terms from his Ohio district. Their long correspondence petered out because of distance or neglect on one side or the other. For Joseph, Westmont had always been "Westy." But the letter he received breaking a silence that lasted between 1982 and 1998 began: "Dear Westmont." Westmont hurriedly wrote back to his longtime friend, beginning, after thinking the matter through, "My dear old friend Joe."

Westmont and the Bear

Timothy Westmont had come to St. Louis for a conference of fellow university-based archivists. By 1998, he was at the end of his career and really had no desire to attend these things any more, but after a long winter in his Indiana college town he was feeling a little stir crazy. Besides, he wanted to get something out of his hands, and maybe even off his conscience, that had been bothering him for a long time. The conference gave him an excuse to follow up a strange phone call he'd received some weeks before. The trip would also give him a chance to see an old friend.

Westmont had come by some interesting materials through his relationship with a member of his school's English department, a certain Kenneth Cobin who had for many years been telling the world, or at least all of his professional colleagues, about a very long biography of William Faulkner that he was preparing. Cobin was in fact a kind of fraud, having conned the department into a salary which, for the 1960s and '70s, was stratospheric—about double the amount paid to an ordinary professor. His job was to put Westmont's college on the map. Although there were no endowed chairs in those days at the college, Cobin was known as the Faulkner Professor of Literature. He relished both the unofficial title and the big time salary, but he never, in fact, finished his book. Some people thought he never even began it. Still, he was a ferocious collector of Faulkner materials. Westmont had often visited the basement bunker in Cobin's house where all the files were kept. This, of course, was in the days before computers, so everything was on paper—handwritten letters and crudely-typed pages going back to the 1920s—and a lot of it was going brown, fading, or actually starting to fall apart; much of the collection badly needed the attention of a professional in conservation. Cobin had filing cabinets flush around all four walls of his bunker, and the long drawers drew out slowly and grandly like the safe-deposit strongboxes in bank vaults. Each drawer was stuffed to the gills with papers and notes. Westmont wondered at once if such an enormous collection of materials could ever be synthesized into a narrative. As an oral storyteller, Cobin was more than impressive. Any scrap that he proudly pulled out to exhibit had its anecdotal history that went on and on in Cobin's vivid and obsessive telling. But Westmont wondered how many pages it would take to write all the stories down in a book. He also wondered how much all the stuff in Cobin's basement might be worth.

On the plane to St. Louis, Westmont was thinking about the former college archive intern with whom he was going to have dinner. Edward Vance was a kind of monastic lapsed Catholic whose bad luck with women paralleled Westmont's own. In fact, Westmont had introduced him to his last two lady friends, both of whom had eventually dropped him, and both of whom wrote books about him, one in the form of a memoir, the other in a collection of "confessional" poems. Though Westmont's wife, like several of her predecessors in his narrow bed, had also left him, at least she wasn't a writer. No one wrote poems about Westmont. At this point in his life, long after his wife returned to her native England, he was seeing no women, as he said in his old-fashioned and ambiguous way, "socially." He wondered if it was the same with Vance.

As the plane descended over the Mississippi, Westmont didn't think about Huck Finn's idyllic river, but the floods and tempests of 1927 and a convict riding through it all in a skiff with a pregnant woman he had rescued from a tree frantic in the bow—scenes from Faulkner's story, *Old Man*. How predictable, how entirely automatic were his associations as he landed in a city on the way to a collapse worthy of Detroit. He yawned to make his ears pop, and shook the cobwebs out of his head. Bring on the millennium, he thought; at least it can't be any worse than our strange little *fin de siècle*. Faulkner got through the Depression writing for the movies. Westmont's depression came with a lower case d—not a big one as in Detroit. After beating off a full-scale breakdown in his late forties, he had fared pretty well until his wife had taken off shortly after his fifty-sixth birthday. Then, slowly, a general melancholy again overtook him, and he had been feeling ghastly for about two years. Nonetheless, he thought of what he was carrying in his briefcase, and it made him smile.

Vance was his usual urbane and cordial self. He was waiting just outside the security area when Westmont passed through. Although he was himself pushing sixty, Vance looked a good twenty years younger than his former supervisor in the archive. In fact, there were only eight years between them. Vance was also very tall. It had always annoyed Westmont that he had to look up at him in order to meet his eye. Only a few years before, Vance had told him that he was "still growing," having gained half an inch after his forty-fifth birthday. In Vance's company Westmont was in fact inclined to look around at the view, whatever it happened to be, or stare at his feet. Still, they were very alike in other ways. Vance used to say about the research that they sometimes had in common that they both read very narrowly but very deep. For Westmont, this was certainly true at the moment. He was only reading William Faulkner.

Vance had known Kenneth Cobin, and had in fact been his student as an undergraduate at Westmont's college. Westmont remembered that when years ago he had asked Vance what Cobin's teaching had been like, the answer was "anecdotal." Cobin would evidently get to a point in a

Faulkner novel or story when he would remember some conversation he'd had with the great man—"just acquaintances," he always said, "not really friends"—and the anecdotes would begin. Very soon the text would be left behind as one memory followed another and Cobin substituted his own stories about "WF," as he called him, and the writings of Faulkner himself were left behind.

"So it was very digressive?" Westmont had asked.

"Very regressive," Vance had replied. "And repetitive, of course. Everyone knew that Cobin was starting to lose his marbles."

That had been more than thirty years ago. Westmont had also been aware that Cobin was starting to lose it back in the Sixties. He remembered in particular one night when he was having drinks with Cobin down in the vault when Cobin had a kind of momentary block he had trouble getting out of. When he didn't call Faulkner "WF" he called him simply "Him." Westmont had seen notes that Cobin had made to himself scattered around the house that said things like "What X said to Him when he met Him in Hollywood," or "Why Y punched Him in the face in 1932." Sometimes, of course, "Him" became "He" or "His" depending on the syntactical requirements of the notes. What had happened that particular night was that Westmont had distinctly heard Cobin refer to "Hem" rather than "Him." This happened a couple of times, and Westmont decided to query it. "Hem?" he asked. Cobin gave him a kind of blank look. Then he said, "You know—that's what his friends all called him. All his friends used to call WF Hem." Westmont had said, "Surely that's what people called Ernest Hemingway." Cobin stared at him for what seemed an unnervingly long time, eyes glazed and unable to speak. When he did finally speak, he didn't pick up the thread, but simply asked Westmont if he wanted another glass of bourbon. There were no further slips and so Westmont chalked the awkward moment up to heavy drinking.

Walking to Vance's car in the airport parking lot, Westmont asked how things were going. "Can't complain," said Vance, "though of course I do. It's hard to get the big bucks to buy up what I want. But of course you warned me about all that many years ago." Westmont said: "No big donors down here?" And Vance just sniffed and shook his head. When they reached the car, an ancient Datsun from another era, Vance drove them to the Vietnamese restaurant where he himself went to dinner every night. He was greeted there as if he were a member of the family. Without even bringing a menu, the waitress served Vance and Westmont spring rolls and white wine and, after that, brought in an order for two of Chicken Almond Ding. Vance explained that she brought them what the management assumed he'd want since his order never varied. If Westmont wanted something else, he'd have to speak up fast. Westmont said that Chicken Almond Ding was fine by him.

They fell into conversation about Kenneth Cobin. Both of them had been attracted to Cobin's young wife when they were working together at Westmont's college in the Sixties. Candida Cobin was easily twenty-five years younger than her husband and had been considered the great beauty in the graduate class that Cobin taught before he left Boston University for Tarkington College. She had tried to make herself look older in those days by dressing in styles from the Fifties, but that had not put off the younger faculty or even the students. Vance said that at his dorm it was the received opinion that Candi Cobin "was a faculty wife who could be had." Westmont himself, married in those days to his English wife, had difficulty paying full attention to Kenneth Cobin and his Faulkner stories when Candida was also around. He thought, in fact, that she was giving signs that she might be available. Her Fifties cashmere sweaters were worn tight against her narrow breasts as he remembered cheerleaders from his high school wearing them. He thought it must have been on purpose when she brushed her thighs against his knee when asking if he's like another piece of quiche at a kind of high tea the Cobins served to friends and acquaintances they thought might be anglophiles.

Westmont was no anglophile, and he was always a little surprised that Cobin was. Cobin was always thrilled to entertain Westmont's wife, who claimed that his affected English accent was as good as anything she'd heard at home when it was still fashionable to talk like a duke in England. Perhaps it played well in Mississippi where Cobin often traveled. There was no doubt that he could be charming, and maybe all those southerners he dealt with in what he called the Faulkner Industry were impressed by his totally achieved persona. He had been known to charm the socks off little old Mississippi ladies who might have Faulkner memorabilia or, even better, manuscripts. His nose for the latter was legendary. He swore he could literally smell them. Once driving by a house not far from Oxford, he slammed on his breaks, stopped the car, and asked at the door if William Faulkner had ever spent any time inside. The faded southern belle said that in fact he had, and more than that she eventually admitted that she had "some papers." Cobin practically drooled. Identifying himself as the Faulkner Professor of Literature from Tarkington College, he asked to see them. Three hours later he left the old lady after drinking tea, sherry, and whisky—in that order and in increasing quantities—for a couple of hours. By then she was not only drunk but in love with him. He had written her a check for $100 and left with a manuscript under his arm—a holograph of pages 176-189 of the first printing of *The Town* that constituted a radically different text from the one in the book.

"Cobin, you know, only talked to Faulkner about horses and flying," said Vance. "He was smart enough to stay off the topic of literature."

"Did you ever go up with him?" asked Westmont.

"What do you mean?"

"You know, up in his plane. Because Faulkner was a pilot, Cobin had to get himself a pilot's license, too. Thought of himself, like WF, as a would-be ace from the First World War, up there with the Red Barron or something. One day I ran into him at the airport after a trip and he insisted that I go flying with him on the spot in the little Cessna he rented. As I'd had a couple of drinks on the incoming flight, I was stupid enough to agree. He nearly killed both of us. I don't know how many hours of instruction he'd had at that point, but he clearly shouldn't have been allowed to fly without supervision, let alone with a passenger. We got off the ground only with about ten yards of the runway left, then flipped and flopped and dipped and dove all the hell over the Midwest for an hour. He kept telling me not to worry, that he knew what he was doing. When I begged him to land, he said he didn't really know where we were, but that we had plenty of fuel. I just shut my eyes and prayed. Toward the end, I heard him say on his radio, "I've got a free balloon at two o'clock." I opened my eyes and, yes indeed, there was a beautiful hot-air balloon, bright blue with orange stripes, and a group of four in the basket waving to us as if the balloon and the Cessna were sailing yachts on a lake in a gentle breeze, and we were all perfectly safe. I shut my eyes again, pretty sure that Cobin would fly the plane straight into the thing, sending us down to earth in a ball of flame or into bursts of black Hun archie coming at us up behind the tracers—stuff that Cobin used to say that WF was taught to fear during his Vickers training, or whatever it was, traversing a Lewis gun on its quadrant. In fact, he got us back with a bit of a bump and made the landing. As we walked to our cars back at the airport he shook his head and told me that WF was a decent pilot but his younger brother wasn't—that the brother had in fact died in a crash and Faulkner suffered terrible guilt for the rest of his life for getting him started in flying."

"Did you ever make it with Candi?" asked Vance.

"What?"

"Were you ever intimate with his wife?"

"Oh, God no. Not that I wasn't tempted. But they really seemed something like newly-weds when we met them. Cobin had plucked her from his graduate class only a year or so before coming to the college. In spite of her flirting with everyone, I still had the sense at first that there might have been a real chemistry between them. Now I rather doubt it. All that dressing up to look like a woman of his own generation seemed like an act of generosity but could just as easily have been a kind of ironic put down. Who knows? She could have made herself look like an undergraduate woman in one of his own classes."

"Well, she fucked my roommate," said Vance.

"What?"

"Yes. The Cobins were over one night for a 'Prof in the Dorm' evening, and Cobin was going on and on with his anecdotes. After a few drinks, Candi made it clear that she'd enjoy seeing my room. Up we went, to the 16th floor—Cobin still down in the lounge and droning on. When we got to the room, I was completely impotent. My roommate, the prescient one who had said long ago that she was 'a faculty wife who could be had,' took over—whispering in my ear, 'well if you don't want to, do you mind if I have a go.' You got used to phrases like 'have a go' if you spent any time with the Cobins. What are you doing here, Westy?" he suddenly asked.

Westmont wasn't sure how much he wanted to tell his old friend. He wasn't fully certain what was going on himself. A few weeks before he decided to make the trip to St. Louis, he had received a call from someone who, without any identification, said in a hushed voice: 'You've got something we want,' and then hung up. Westmont assumed this was a crank call and forgot about it. The next day, at exactly the same time, he received the same call with the same message. The third day, before proceeding to 'You've got something we want,' the voice said: 'I'm a friend of Ikkemotubbe.' This time Westmont sat up with a start. When the phone went dead, he asked the college operator if there were a way to trace the number. There was not. After that, the calls came several times a day, and the caller added, bit by bit, more information.

"Well," said Westmont, "I got a call from Ikkemotubbe."

"From Ike who?"

"Ikkemotubbe," said Westmont. "Or, as it turned out, from his representative. It was a woman's voice. She had been calling me for a few days and saying, very politely, 'You've got something we want.'"

"But Ike who? What are you talking about?"

"Don't you remember at the beginning of WF's private mythology? There's a Chickasaw called Ikkemotubbe who sells some land to Thomas Sutpen for a bottle of rum or something. It ends up in the hands of Carothers McCaslin, and then his descendents screw everything up."

"No, I don't remember any of that," said Vance. "It's been a long time."

It didn't seem such a long ago time to Westmont. *The Bear*. What a fine piece of work; he and Cobin certainly agreed on that. And what a treat for an archivist was the fourth section of the great story he knew so well when all those complicated genealogies are explained, and one is made acquainted with Carothers and Major de Spain and Tennie Beauchamp and Perival Brownlee and Scottish McCaslin forbears going all the way back to Culloden, and slave-girl lovers and mixed-race siblings and cousins and daughters and sons and grandkids, and Sam Fathers' fathers and General Compson's exploits and Boon Hogganbeck's Chickasaw way with Lion the mongrel dog, all coming forward right down to the present. He had loved all that and shared that love with Cobin. And then eventually he heard that when Cobin taught the story to his undergraduates he told them to skip part IV altogether and go right on to part V. At first he thought that Cobin wanted to keep certain things to himself, just to savor on his own, or perhaps with the fully initiated. However, as Cobin's problems with drinking and his memory progressed, Westmont began to think that the complexities of these things had become difficult for Cobin to talk about, that in fact he had begun to forget first the complex genealogies and then even some of the WF plots, convoluted as they were. He felt sorry and embarrassed for Cobin, but he also understood by the early 1970s that it was getting time for him to make his move.

Once he started taking things, it seemed remarkably easy. Cobin, growing more and more vague as the evening and the drinking progressed, would finally fall asleep on his leather sofa, his head slumping onto his chest. When Westmont left, Candida would sometimes still be up and doing things on the main floor of the house. She'd ask, "has he fallen asleep again?" and then say: "Oh never mind, I'll get him up to bed in a while." There were times when Westmont thought Candida was even secretly complicit in what became his increasingly regular and finally compulsive thefts. One year, at a party for Westmont's fortieth birthday, she and Cobin gave him a rare and valuable copy of the May 1888 edition of *The Atlantic* containing Henry James' story, *The Aspern Papers*, all about conniving to get at the private correspondence of a famous

American poet based on the figure of Byron. Westmont thought he saw a fleeting smirk on Candi's face as Cobin said loudly: "For the college archive, or for you yourself. Whichever you like is fine with us."

He kept it for himself in a filing cabinet much like those he admired in Cobin's vault. In the same cabinet he had already placed many Faulkner items stolen from Cobin's collection as Cobin drifted into an evening's alcoholic daze. Cobin's slowly progressing dementia made it increasingly easy over the years to relieve him of many invaluable papers, letters, privately printed limited editions, and sometimes just curiosities—one of WF's rejected pipes, a couple of screws from a bridal bit, buttons from a coat he had worn in Stockholm when they gave him the big prize. He wouldn't have been surprised to discover in Cobin's collection actual relics: fingernail clippings, say, or a vial of WF's Sangreal.

Vance was saying something about the Mississippi. In all his years in St. Louis, he'd never been down to the banks. It was just like him, he said, and he was sure that if he had lived in Paris he'd never notice the Eiffel Tower. He and his old mentor would rather read about something in a book than experience the thing itself. Laughing, he remembered how they years ago admitted to each other their preference for a good book of prints to an art gallery visit, a performance on CD to an actual concert. But Westmont wasn't taking this in. He was drifting on a WF text that he had long had by heart, the very holy writ of his existence, his creed, his dream, his bliss: *To him it was as though the ledgers in their scarred cracked leather bindings were being lifted down one by one in their fading sequence and spread open on the desk or perhaps upon some apocryphal Bench or even Altar or perhaps before the Throne Itself for a last perusal and contemplation and refreshment of the All Knowledgeable before the yellowed pages and the brown thin ink in which was recorded the injustice and a little at least of its amelioration and restitution faded back forever into the anonymous communal original dust...*

"Westy," Vance said, "have you heard a single word that I've been saying?"

After dinner, Vance drove him to the Tudor Suites Hotel. As Westmont was entirely unacquainted with the geography of the city, he didn't have much sense of where they were going, but it seemed to be only a ten or fifteen minute drive from the restaurant. Vance apologized for the theme park look of the hotel. "Inside," he said, "you'll find torches lining the halls—really more like a medieval castle than anything Tudor, but they try their best. The rooms are perfectly comfortable and it's not far from the campus." Westmont looked uneasily at the Disneyland turrets and ramparts with a sinking heart. He'd been put up in places like this before. Giving Vance an awkward hug from his seat in the car, he said they'd see each other the next day. Vance waved from his window as he drove away.

Once inside the Tudor Suites, he saw the torches at once—some kind of flickering electronic vulgarities on free-standing posts leading down three hallways extending at odd angles from the entrance hall. The walls were covered with phony tapestries representing banquets, jousts and famous portraits of Henry VIII and Elizabeth. There was nobody there but a lady behind the desk watching a small TV. Westmont identified himself and was given the key and told that his room was 184, down the hall to his left. "Have a great day," the receptionist said, going back to her program. A few steps from the desk was the entrance to the hotel bar and just outside a large sign saying:

HAPPY HOUR, 5:00—7:30 EVERY DAY
EVEN SUNDAYS

He had a look inside. There was just one customer, sipping a drink. At the back of the room, beyond some tables and adjacent to a gas-log fire blazing away, even though it was still warm and not yet October, was a towering stuffed animal—a bear.

The sight of the bear gave Westmont a shock. He was not prepared for this. Walking quickly down the hall to his room, he fumbled with the key, dropped it once—it was a real key, a large one, and not a piece of plastic—and finally managed to let himself into the room. When he shut the door, he leaned against it briefly as if he were expecting someone to pursue him down the hall and force an entry. Then he threw himself onto the enormous king-size double bed. Lying there, he thought about Delmore in his suitcase. How could he not, given the Ben-sized work of some evil taxidermist in the bar. Good old Delmore. Good old Delmore and terrifying Ben, the two extremes of his ursine universe. But he hadn't counted on such proximity. He heaved himself from the bed and opened his suitcase. There was Delmore, small and sweet and almost bald from head to foot, and very, very old. There had been a time, in Columbus, when Delmore had endured a very traumatic experience. Outside his mother's nursing home, Westmont had opened his car door in such a way that Delmore fell onto the asphalt parking lot. Not having noticed this, Westmont drove to his motel. Once he realized that Delmore was missing, he had returned to the nursing home and looked and looked and looked. In the end, he was forced to ring the night-staff bell and ask if anyone had found a bear in the parking lot. Luckily, they had. The young nurse asked: "Brown, and kind of hairless?" Westmont said: "That's him." Then there had been an embarrassed exchange of smiles as Westmont recovered his companion and the nurse locked up for the night. He took Delmore from the suitcase, fluffed up a pillow on the king-size bed, and placed the bear upon his nighttime guard-post.

Delmore was a gift from Westmont's estranged wife. At some point a couple of decades earlier Westmont had begun to show signs of depression, agoraphobia, and hypochondria. It all became worse the year a tree fell through the front room roof and window during a bad windstorm. For months before the storm, Westmont had been spending more and more time in the archive, coming home late at night and making himself drinks before falling into bed like a dead man only to wake up in a panic, sometimes shouting out and flailing his arms and legs, two or three hours later. After that he couldn't sleep at all, and so he added chronic insomnia to his list of ills when he visited the several doctors he was seeing on a regular basis. When he added a psychiatrist to his cocktail of specialists, things started getting difficult for Sally. At some point along the way, Westmont had alluded to his remembered affection for a childhood cocker spaniel, Buffy. "For God's sake, Westy," Sally had said on the third or fourth occasion he'd mentioned the dog with fond nostalgia, "why don't you go out and get another bloody hound. Or maybe a teddy bear. Either one would probably interest you more than I seem to these days." A week or so after her outburst, Sally returned from a trip to the shopping mall with Delmore. "Here," she said, "This is for you." And with that she took her pillows and reading lamp and moved to the back bedroom.

Delmore was named for the American *poète maudit*, Delmore Schwartz. Even this had a connection with Cobin who had once been a colleague of Schwartz's when they were both briefly at Harvard. This was in the days of Delmore's early fame when he was writing poems that had long since fallen out of the anthologies like the one Sally was thinking of when she brought back her gift, and ultimately her parting shot, from the shopping mall. "The heavy bear that goes with me" she sang, making Delmore dance in the air by holding up his front legs and bouncing him on her lap. That was a line that Cobin liked to quote as well—in fact it was the only reason Sally remembered it at all—mocking people who were, unlike his tall, svelte self, a little overweight. Westmont was overweight, which was in part a result of drinking so much with Cobin.

But Cobin, before he lost it mentally, showed no physical damage from his heavy drinking and his liking for heavy French sauces on most of what he ate. As for the original Delmore, he dismissed him as a poet and called him "an unfortunate neurotic" and "hopelessly unprofessional," someone who had ended up as "a wholly grotesque wreck."

Westmont was certainly feeling all those things himself when the companion now propped on the pillow of the Tudor Suite's king size bed had arrived on the scene—neurotic, unprofessional, a wreck. And it had actually helped having Delmore along for company. Once he began to recover a little from his funk—and especially when Sally had returned to her native England and left him alone—Delmore simply had become an accustomed part of his life.

But then there was Ben—WF's Old Ben, a kind of ursine Moby Dick. "Bear thou never wert," Westmont recited to himself, though in the story Ben seemed real enough both in his terrible rage and pitiful fall. Westmont had once tried to place him on the zoological map, but clearly Ben was meant to be of Cave Bear stature, some Ursa Major out of the sky, and not even Grizzlies roamed in Mississippi during the time WF was living or writing about, let alone the creature depicted on cave walls in the Ardèche some thirty-five thousand years ago. Mississippi was the habitat of roly-poly black bears, and Ben was to them as Melville's Great Whale was to goldfish. In fact, Mississippi was the original home of the Teddy Bear—Theodore Roosevelt having refused on a 1902 hunting expedition there to shoot one of the black bears caught by a retainer and offered to the president like a criminal to a firing squad. "Let him go," said TR, and the merciful gesture became international news. Soon after, "Teddy's Bear" made an appearance at the Leipzig Toy Show and, mass-produced by Borgfeldt & Co., took the world by storm leading eventually to, well, Delmore.

In the midst of Westmont's reveries, his telephone rang. Half asleep, he picked it up and said hello.

"I'm here," a woman's voice said. "Meet me in the bar."

Westmont had no time to reply as the phone immediately went dead. He got out of bed, went into the bathroom and bathed his face for a moment in cold water. After drying it, and combing what remained of his hair, he stared for a moment at his drawn face in the mirror. Then he picked up his briefcase and key and left for the bar.

At first there was nobody there, not even a bar tender. Westmont stared at the taxidermied creature at the far end of the lounge. It was enormous. Clearly more than eight feet tall, it had been frozen forever the very way that large trophy bears usually are—roaring with its mouth wide open, its great teeth bared, standing at its full height with front legs reaching out like human arms and the razor-sharp claws extended and ready to tear any enemy's flesh from its bones with a single swipe of a paw. Westmont slowly approached the creature. As he got closer, he realized that its coat was tattered, like an old fur garment left hanging for years in somebody's closet. Large patches looked to have been eaten away by moths or termites. Something was leaking out of these wounds, a kind of dust, and there were small piles of this discharge on the floor beneath him. His eyes looked more sad than ferocious, as if he were embarrassed to be presented to the world as an embodiment of fury. Westmont reached forward and gave him a pat on the side. "Poor Bear," he said aloud.

"But incorruptible," answered a voice behind him.

Westmont turned around. Just inside the door was a very handsome black woman dressed in an expensive-looking business suit with what looked like an artist's portfolio under her left arm and carrying a drink with tinkling ice cubes in her right hand.

"Incorruptible," she said again, "but fallen. And yet immortalized as art there before your eyes. Lo, he stands as if alive! You'll remember the fall yourself—the clinging dog called "Lion," the bear, the man Boon astride with his knife plunged into the ursine heart... all falling together, falling as a tree falls, like a piece of classic statuary, asunder, asunder, Crash! Poor bear. Can I buy you a drink?" She motioned to one of the tables at the still, except for them, entirely empty lounge. It was late, after all. Westmont sat down, not saying a word.

"What will you have," she continued. "I'll bet bourbon. Like Massa William F." Out of nowhere a bartender arrived with a bourbon and ice on a tray beside a carafe of water. She took the water for herself and passed the bourbon to Westmont. "Cheers," she said with a smile.

Westmont took a sip of his drink. "*Who* are you?" he asked. "Are you the person who phoned me in Indiana?"

"Well," she said, "that's two questions, ain't it? I's the one that phoned, but as to *Who I is*, that's damn complicated. Issetibbeha's sister's son done sol' my grandpappy up de river, boss, instead of down, which was when l'Frog Chevalier Sueur-Blonde de Vitry called him *Man, Du Homme*, and finally, like it's said in Massa's books, Englished it as *Doom*. My own mum was injun-nigger-froggy in some mix, she never really got it straight, but anyway she married or just lived in sin with, I forget, the grandson of some former slave who owned a farm but didn't cultivate the land, just sat on his porch and read his Frederick Douglas books and, all in God's good time, wrote an unpublished how-to-do-it guide about the best ways to capture people wont to burglarize the archives, purloin the letters as it were, of other folks. But you know all that shit, Bro, don't you now."

Westmont stared at her. She was no longer smiling. "Who *are* you?" he asked again. "You haven't even told me your name."

"Me?" she said. I'm Candi Cobin. Has it been so long that you don't even recognize me? Half a dozen times we nearly ended up in bed, but maybe you don't, after all these years, remember that. Or is it just my black sister-lady total-method overmake? I'll grant you it was pretty damn expensive. I've not just been tanning, baby, this is permanent. Ain't just either only bout my face, Mr. Westwhatever. Like to see some more?" She made a gesture of reaching for the buttons on her blouse. "Tits are also black, you handsome hunk, but let's get down to business," and she picked the portfolio up from the floor and put it on the table.

"What the hell do you mean that you're Candida Cobin?" Westmont asked.

"Westy, I was puttin' you on, Old Boy, Old Chap. A joke, Mon Vieux. I guess I've been thinking about this thing long enough that ah jus *feels* like Candi Cobin."

"How do you know Mrs. Cobin?"

"To Ben!" she said, ignoring his question. And she toasted the taxidermied bear with her glass of water. "My friend," she said, giving him a straight look. "Want to see some dirty pictures?" She opened up the portfolio and began thumbing through the loose-leaf pages inside and taking half a dozen out that she placed face down on Westmont's side of the table.

"Turn over the first card," she said.

"Is this some kind of game?"

"Just turn it over, please."

Westmont turned over the first of the large and stiff papers in front of him.

"Snap!" she said. "*Juan del Oso, Gian dell'Orso*. In whichever language you like, the bear is nursing a human child along with her cubs. Folk tale, Bro, told in many tongues. Kind of like the Roman wolf you learned about in Latin class. I've not got a *Westmont de l'ours* picture-perfect portrait here, but we do know he exists in the wild somewhere off in France or Indiana. Turn over the next card."

Westmont did so.

"Snap!" she said. "Greek vase. Callisto's hand now turneth into paw. Mustn't make the goddess angry, right? Furious Artemis. Do take care for whom thou list to hunt, for she doth know all hinds and every species of bear."

"See here," said Westmont. "What's this all about?"

"Bears," she said. "Turn another card."

He did.

"Snap!" she said. "Tibet. The creature's stuffed, much like our friend Benjamin right here. The natives think they've captured Yeti, known to you as the abominable snowman I should guess, brought down from the highest mountain peak and executed in an ancient bloody ritual. Nasty, Mr. Eastprick-Westcunt, very nasty those Tibetans. Now I think I'll play a card myself. You say what it is. I've got a hunch you're going to know."

When she turned it over, Westmont took in his breath quite audibly. It was an enlarged photograph of himself with Candida and Kenneth Cobin, taken probably in the early 1970s. They were in the basement vault, all drinking bourbon, naturally. Cobin was wearing his proprietary look, his hand on a manuscript or first edition. Westmont himself looked uncertain, a half-smile on his lips, his bourbon glass held up in a kind of half-toast to the photographer. Candi looked—available. He supposed his wife had taken the photograph, as she did not herself appear in it.

"Of course I recognize it," Westmont said. "Where did you get it, anyway?"

"Snap!" she said. "And now try this."

The photograph showed an old man in a wheelchair being pushed by a middle-aged woman. The man had the leonine expression of a person with dementia, but it was clearly Cobin. Slumped in the wheelchair, he was not looking at the camera but beyond it, as if trying to make something out in the distance. The angle of the photograph was wide enough to show an institutional context; people on canes and walkers looked distractedly in the direction of the photographer.

"Is Candida pushing that chair?" asked Westmont.

"*Bien sûr*, Big Sir", she said. "Ghastly hellhole, don't you think? In the end the world's nothing but a fucking ward for fucking gaga Gagas. Ever visited a locked floor for Altzies? Give up hope all Ye who enter there. *Nel mezzo del cammin di nostra vita* and all that, you know, except it wasn't in poor Cobin's case the middle but the end. He never left, once he was committed. Candi didn't take him anywhere but up and down the hall. Eventually, poor things, they don't know who you are, even if you're married to them. They positively *freak* when they look at themselves in a mirror. The long halls have indirect lighting because their own shadow, if they were to see it, would make them fucking bloody panic. But you, of course…"

"I know," he said, "my mother…"

"Forgive me," she said. "I acknowledge dear old mum, although you hardly ever went to see her. Died all alone, did she not? Died in your absence. Some nurse talking on the phone and saying 'This is what we see… pitting nails, dilated pupils. Just so you know.' I was told by a mutual acquaintance how Ms. Candi had to boo-hoo hold your hand through all of that, your spouse having left by then your needful side for her own native green and pleasant land."

"There was a blizzard," he pleaded. "I couldn't make the drive."

"Here's another card," she said. "Can you snap?"

A very old man stood by a mound of earth beside a shack. He was very black. The photograph wasn't properly focused and was damaged by a fold mark down the center. You couldn't see the man's expression at all. In the background, miles and miles of cotton fields. Was this something from the Civil War? A Brady picture, maybe? Westmont stared. Behind the old man, trying unsuccessfully to hide, was a little girl. You could barely make her out, peeping around the old man's hip. She was ten, twelve years old.

"Me and Granpappy," said the woman. "And I'd never in this world expect you to recognize the two of us. But, you know, there was this one weird night. Your old friend Cobin came to dig. That's right, dig. Right in our back yard. He said he'd got it figured Massa William F done give a hint in what he wrote that Old Ben's actual-factual hurt and amputated paw was buried near the bodies of the old original for Sam Fathers and the mutt terrier of crazy Boon that he done wrote about and then that Cobin wrote about eventually as well. What, baby, has you got for me in that official-looking briefcase? Although you ain't no lawyer, White Man, I am, and I'm here to tell you that I represent a client that you know and an estate. Shall we play a bit more "Snap!" or shall we just quote some bits of Massa F? I've always liked the open drawer in that *Sartoris* where the reader *sees a shotgun shell to which was attached by a piece of wire a withered bear's paw.* But that's not quite got it right because it's early writing and the later version in the famous tale has it that when Ike McCaslin dug a little into granpappy's garden as it would become once all the loggers left and once the railroad men had cut the trees to lay their rails he found a round box *manufactured for axle-grease and containing now Old Ben's dried mutilated paw, resting above Lion's bones.* Lion was the furious Airedale mutt, gutted by the bear, but nonetheless the dog that brought him down. Ike or his original had enough respect to bless the relic and rebury it. As well Massa Faulkner when he came later on and had a look. But not our friend your former colleague Cobin with that bloodhound nose of his. You know," she continued, "that bourbon drinking anglophile of a scholar dug around this place of grandpappy's in the night like some possessed Flem Snopes. What he found and took back to his lair he regarded as a true and actual relic—that part, my Westerdexter, of the old martyr's paw that got snapped off in some Boon Hogganbottom of a trap and left him Two-toe Oedipus the cripple-foot whose tracks distinguished him for years from the prey that ordinary hunters sought. All them swamp rats with them lighted pine-knot torches knowing when to show up every year for decades just to watch. And what a show it was. I know what you're going to say—it's just a story, some kind of trick mimetic gimmick, but to me, a Beauchamp myself from what the Massa called the distaff side of things—which means I turned out black—I know what you've got inside that briefcase ain't no *trompe l'oeil*, is it now? But what, do you think, it really is?

"Who is your client?" Westmont asked.

"Mr. Wasteblossom," she said. "I'm pretty sure you've guessed the answer to that. Then she tapped loudly with her forefinger on the bare part of the table between their two stacks of enlarged photographs. "It's time you let me see the friggin thing."

He reached in his briefcase and took it out. It looked like a withered piece of beef jerky pierced by the sharp end of a paperclip and attached by that mechanism to a deeply rusted shotgun shell. They both stared at it in silence.

"It's not very impressive, is it?" she said.

"No, not very."

She looked up and smiled at him. "But even so, we can take this as a token that you relinquish the rest of it?"

"Relinquish?" he said.

"The rest of it. He really was obsessive about this stuff, wasn't he? Ever been to the Vatican in Rome?" she asked. "This would fit right in. They've got pigs' bones they say come from the saints, and bits of horse tails called the Virgin's pubic hair."

"Will this go to court?" he asked.

"Not unless you want it to, Mr. Westmont, provided you follow our instructions. The firm will be in touch with you by ordinary mail. There will be a few forms to fill in. Not much more than that. If you were to contest even a single aspect of the charges against you, well—it could get ugly."

"Will I hear anything from Candi?"

"Who knows?" she said. "I kind of doubt it."

"I remember her as a really good-looking woman."

"A good-looking woman."

"Yes. A really good-looking woman."

"Mr. Westmont, I must be off. It's been pleasant doing business with you." She picked up the bear's toe, paper-clipped to the shotgun shell, and stood up abruptly. Then she reached forward to shake hands with Westmont. An elegant hand, he noticed—long tapered fingers and professionally manicured nails. He wondered what a scratch from her would feel like. More like a cat's than a bear's.

Then she was off, disappearing quickly out the open door of the hotel bar. Westmont sat alone for a while sipping his by now very watery bourbon. So that was that. Why did people save things, anyway? In the end, everything was more or less lost. He remembered an old friend of his who had been famous in his day in the field of physics. Westmont had urged him to leave his papers in the archive. But his friend had shredded everything, even letters from Einstein and Niels Bohr. "In the end," his friend had told him, "nobody cares. No one comes to read the stuff." Perhaps he was right. Westmont finished up his drink, stood up, saluted the pathetic, leaking trophy-bear—who, after all, couldn't have been Ben, who lived only in a work of fiction. But just for fun he stepped forward and looked carefully at all four paws just to make sure. All the toes were there. Then he slowly walked back to his room. The light on his telephone was blinking. Doubtless a message from Vance. He pushed the button and listened.

"Hi, Westy. A slight change in the schedule. The 2:30 panel is cancelled, so you and I will substitute and at 4:30 we'll go straight to cocktails. I'll sing your praises for a little, then you can say whatever you like about old Cobin. Might as well be really basic with the info since most people here won't remember anything about him. Great to catch up at dinner. Cheers."

There was also a second message. He pushed the button.

"This is Candida Cobin speaking. I know it's been years, but I'm glad this thing is going to be settled. Miss Tabitha is rather a tough cookie, I'm afraid. But, as I'm sure she let you know, one way or another, she's kind of a family member now. You know something else? I absolutely can't stand William Faulkner, and I never could. As far as I'm concerned, you could keep all that loot you took if I didn't need some ready cash. I'm told there won't be money for this stuff forever—literary study being on the outs—so I've got to act before it disappears entirely. Sorry to have made a nuisance of myself. Hugs from me in far-off California. I do sometimes miss our old times together."

He put down the telephone.

"Well," said Westmont, picking Delmore up and holding him high in the air. "It's been a rather difficult day. Why don't you and I just skip the conference and see if we can find ourselves a flight back home as early in the morning as you can manage to wake up? They've been rather unpleasant to us here, don't you think? For now, it's all lights out, and let's have a long and happy sleep."

Westmont and the Different Kinds of Music

4

After a very stimulating spring term in advanced English seminar taught by a student teacher substituting for Mr. Bateman, Westmont asked the assistant principal in the following fall term what had become of Mr. Glabb. It seemed that Mr. Glabb had graduated and was now teaching high school full-time in town. Westmont told the assistant principal, Mr. Jennings, how good a teacher Mr. Glabb had been, better, he confided, than Mr. Bateman himself. (All the boys, of course, called the latter Master Bateman behind his back.) Mr. Jennings was a little surprised to hear this, but said he would tell Mr. Glabb what Westmont had said and pass along his good wishes. Within a few weeks, Westmont had a letter from Mr. Glabb. It was very formal, addressing him as "Dear Mr. Westmont," and going on to talk at length about what he was teaching at his new school. At the end, he asked Westmont if he would like to meet "for a cup of tea." Westmont had never been invited for "a cup of tea" by anyone, but eagerly wrote back to accept the invitation. Where, he asked in his reply, should they meet? In a few days he got another letter suggesting the Broad Street Coffee Shop at a particular date and time. (Westmont assumed that they must also serve tea there.) Mr. Glabb included a phone number where he could be reached in order to confirm the meeting. Westmont phoned him the next day and they agreed to a time in the late afternoon. When they spoke on the phone, Westmont could hear singing in the background.

Mr. Glabb was fat, breathless, and had a badly repaired harelip that had pulled his lower face into a kind of contorted shape. He was, in fact, so ugly that the students at Westmont's school had been uniformly kind to him, always did their homework promptly, and certainly didn't make up names for him as they did with Mr. Bateman. In fact, it was generally agreed that Mr. Glabb was a "good guy." He could even persuade them to read long novels, like *Moby Dick* (which the students had another name for when Mr. Bateman taught it). Mr. Glabb looked around the classroom and said, "I'm giving you access to something great here, something really great. Don't let me down."

Westmont hadn't let him down. When they met, however, a good deal of time had passed. The "tea" at Broad Street Coffee Shop was a rather strange experience, as Westmont thought it would only be tea in a cup but found himself with a mountain of little sandwiches and cakes to deal with. Also, Mr. Glabb almost immediately asked him if he'd like to attend an opera with him. It would be in Cincinnati at the Zoo. Westmont thought that was a strange place for an opera, but Mr. Glabb explained that in fact the Cincinnati Opera at the Zoo was the second oldest company in America, after the Met. Westmont wasn't sure what the Met was, or for that matter what a "company" was. His father's law firm represented many companies, but this was clearly something else.

They went to the opera together. It was *La Traviata*. During the longish drive to Cincinnati, Mr. Glabb explained the plot. He said the lead character was a "courtesan," but didn't explain what that meant. He also explained something of the soprano's reputation. She was internationally known in that role. The opera house turned out indeed to be located in a zoo. It was an amphitheater with a roof, but with open sides, like Ravinia in Chicago. Westmont tried not to laugh when the seals barked during arias. On the way back, Mr. Glabb put his hand on Westmont's knee. "Are you awake there, Mr. Westmont?" It had been "Mr. Westmont" all day long. He didn't know what to think.

When they got back to Columbus, Mr. Glabb left Westmont where he'd asked to be left, even though it was very late. He knew his friends would be at Johnny's 402 Club listening to jazz. He asked Mr. Glabb if he'd like to come in and hear Ahmad Jamal, who was playing there with his trio. Mr. Glabb said that "it was past the witching hour," but tried to give him a kiss when he got out of the car.

Once inside Johnny's 402 Club, Westmont found his friends around a table at the back. Jamal was taking a break, so everyone was talking loudly. When he walked up to the table, his friend Joel, who had clearly had a few drinks, even though he was under age like everyone else, stuck a finger in Westmont's chest and said: "Westy's been to the opera. With our former English teacher, Mr. Glabb." Everyone laughed as if this was the funniest thing they'd ever heard. David Goss said, "I also heard they'd gone to tea." Again everyone cracked up. Paul Gherhardt said: "The opera! What was it, 'The Magic Fart?'" "No," Westmont said, "It was 'La Traviata.' Last year all you guys thought Mr. Glabb was cool." David Goss said, "Oh, that was last year."

Westmont and Tar Hollow Camp

Westmont hadn't considered himself particularly religious since he had, as they say, grown up. There had been a time, however, between the ages of twelve and fifteen, when his various superstitions—rubbing a smooth stone he had found on a beach, shutting the door three times when he left or entered his bedroom—became something else. It was The Book that had done it, the Holy Bible itself. An aunt on his mother's side of the family had given him for his birthday a copy of *The Westminster Study Edition*, a kind of strict Presbyterian version intended for amateur theologians and keen laymen, that for a while he prized above all his possessions. It was full of what the scholars call apparatus: maps of the Holy Land, a concordance, endless footnotes, introductions to every book, a tactful discussion of theological niceties like justification by faith alone and original sin. In retrospect, Westmont thought it was doubtless the physical object he had loved, not knowing that his wonderful book would be replaced by many others he would find more wonderful still. He didn't read it a lot, not having really become anything like the would-be scholar and bibliophile he would start to resemble in high school, but he thumbed its amazingly thin pages with a kind of awe and began rubbing it, especially after masturbation, once he had lost confidence in his smooth stone. Though no one had actually said so, he knew that the obsessive act he had discovered in bed was somehow wrong, maybe even something connected with the originality of the sin he read about in the *Westminster Study Edition*'s scholia, and so he believed for a while that touching the grand and expensive book instead of the stone a little while after humping his pillow somehow absolved him quickly enough of something he didn't really want to dwell on.

In the summer of his fourteenth year Westmont's parents sent him to a summer camp. Wanting to put off for as long as possible his first prolonged absence from home, Westmont argued for the latest possible of several available two-week sessions at Camp Tar Hollow, a fairly secular and fully co-ed and progressive version of a religious camp run in a valley of the Ohio Hocking Hills by the Main Street Presbyterian Church. Founded decades before on the traditional model of a serious and prolonged religious retreat, Tar Hollow Camp had evolved into a fortnight of baseball, swimming, hiking, and the like. There were morning and evening prayers, some hymn singing, and a famous ritual "bonfire night," but parents were told that it was all mostly for fun and games. Still, each camper was told to bring a Bible.

Westmont—Westy to his parents and friends—never wanted to attend this camp or any other. What he liked to do in the summers was to play with his visiting cousins in the ravine near his home. Robert and Richard shared his enthusiasm for imaginative games. They would all dress up in costumes concocted from a chest full of accessories ranging from his grandfather's Spanish-American war swords and discarded bits of uniform to plumes from women's hats that had gone out of style in the 1920s and 30s. The amazing thing was their ability to sustain the games they played through hours and hours of improvised plot and dialogue. In later life Westmont wondered how they had done it. Once in character, their world of knights or pirates took over so thoroughly that they inhabited it to the exclusion of any intrusion of reality at all. Westmont tried now and then to compare memories with others of his generation about childhood games, but no one else seemed to have played them with the intensity he had. He loved these games, and he loved his cousins because they loved them as well. Sometimes he'd try to get some other child interested in the kind of thing the cousins did together, but no one else seemed to get the idea. A few would try, but with a kind of embarrassment. Finally these other friends would throw down the sword and cape and say—"let's go play ball with the others down the glen."

The glen. Even the word was wrong. Westmont's parents called it "the ravine," not "the glen." But because Old Glen Echo Drive ran through it, everybody else in the neighborhood called it the glen. Westmont was an outsider, and he knew it. He also knew that he was the butt of jokes among the tough kids in his neighborhood because of his summer games with the cousins. In fact, he was often afraid of getting roughed up by those who called him names. One time his cousins didn't tell him he'd forgotten to take off his cowboy hat safety-pinned into a tricorne with a wonderful bright yellow plume until they'd reached Gray's drugstore soda counter and they were all ordering their Cokes. Robert and Richard thought it was a good joke on Westy, but the neighborhood kids browsing the movie and Hot Rod magazines at the store never let him forget it. "Westy," they'd say through the long fall and winter following the cousins' return to Washington, D.C. where they lived, "how's your pirate hat? How about a game of Horatio Hornblower? How about a blow job? How about we break your sissy teeth out?"

Given that the tough kids in the neighborhood had now, as it were, discovered him, it took a certain amount of courage to go down in the ravine in costume. Still, it was there that the best forts, lookouts, and ambush sites could be found. One summer during a bad wind storm the tall cherry tree in his back yard was blown down in such a way that the trunk tilted over the wall at the edge of the family property and many large limbs actually plunged on down the hill into the ravine. Once the storm was over, Westy and his cousins costumed themselves as officers in Lord Nelson's navy and played at boarding enemy ships or abandoning their own in a typhoon or following a ferocious attack by the French. After two days of this, they ventured, still in costume, on down the ravine to continue their game as sailors shipwrecked on a frightening alien shore.

The cousins skipped through many summers down the narrow Glen Echo Drive with the alacrity of Tin Man, Straw Man, and Cowardly Lion tripping along the yellow brick road to look for the Wizard of Oz. But Westmont set off to camp only with a heavy heart and a sense of serious obligation. Richard and Robert had signed up for camps of their own one year—they were two and three years older than he was—and the following year Westmont felt that he had to follow suit. Robert, the oldest cousin, had even said during one of their last games together, "Maybe we're getting a little old for this." It had been clear to Westmont that Robert's improvisational skills had been starting to flag. He could see for himself what was coming. Although he held out for a year, he finally agreed that he would follow Robert and Richard into what was represented to him as a way to meet new friends and learn new skills. But he understood pretty clearly that this was mainly intended as an unwanted initiation into a proper adolescence. He had loved being a child.

Packing up his duffle bag, camping gear and Bible the night before he was scheduled to leave on a church bus for Tar Hollow, Westmont had one moment of real anger, telling his parents that the whole idea of camp was "entirely wrong." His parents laughed at this, finding "entirely" not entirely the kind of adverb they associated with their son's objections to things. And his father also noted: "Wrong is a pretty heavy-duty word, you know. As you've got your Bible with you, look it up in the Concordance." He did: *To him that did the w. Ex. 2:13; I cry out of w. Job 19:7; Friend, I owe thee no w. Mt. 20:13; A matter of w. Acts 18:14; Why do ye not take w. I Cor. 6:7; He that doeth w. Col. 3:25; If he hath w. thee. Phlm. 18.* His eye skipped to Wrath. *Let not the sun go down on your w. Eph. 4: 26.* He turned from this austere scholarship to the list of "Camper Rules." These rules told him that, among other things, his parents were not permitted to visit at all during the two weeks at camp, but that "writing home is encouraged." Campers were to have clean bodies and clothes, swim only at swim periods and only in the swimming area, stay seated in the lodge at meals until everyone was dismissed, report for hopper duty on time, participate in cabin devotions, and never to visit "other hills" than one's own without authorization. Especially boys were forbidden to be on the girls' hill and vice-versa. Miserably, he said goodnight to his parents and went to bed.

The first person he saw on the bus was Buddy Dagger. This was a disaster. Buddy was one of the tough kids in his neighborhood who had taunted Westmont about his costumes and games with his cousins. Once, Buddy even "beat him up" when he had dared to walk through the alley from the Hudson Street movie theater rather than taking the safe but longer route down Summit Street to his home. Buddy lived in a kind of apartment above a garage. It was the only living accommodation that one could actually say fronted on the alley. Westmont had never seen a sign of any Dagger parents, only an older sister who had a reputation for doing strip shows in the empty garage below the flat. Buddy tended to lurk about the place, looking for trouble, and had bloodied the nose of many a younger kid in the neighborhood. In Westmont's case, he had appeared out of nowhere to block Westmont's route to the back door of the Arcadia Avenue side of his house. "Hey, Westy," he'd said. "How about you and me fight it out." "There's nothing to fight about," Westmont had replied, trying to hurry by. "Oh yes there is," said Buddy, and pushed Westmont against a fence. As he tried to regain his balance, Buddy took a wild punch that managed to connect with Westmont's cheekbone, opening a small tear in the skin. That was all, but Westmont maintained that Buddy Dagger had "beaten him up in the alley" and never walked down it again in his life. And here was Buddy also going to camp and sneering at him from the backseat in the bus.

Westmont sat down in the front seat directly behind the driver. He didn't dare turn around to look at Buddy again, but he glanced to his right and allowed his head a kind of three-quarter turn so that he could see down the aisle about half way to the back. He recognized a few kids from church and even one boy from his school, John Dewey Central, which was run by the Department of Education at the college where his father worked by a group of Ph.D.s who saw to it that all of the students understood and appreciated that they were the beneficiaries of a "progressive education." Westmont was as appreciative of this as anyone else, but the school he attended was one of the reasons he was something of a pariah in the neighborhood. Everyone who went to Medary, the local neighborhood school, had strange ideas about John Dewey. Those who didn't think it was a school for mental defectives thought it was for misfit geniuses or the exclusive privilege of academic brats—sons and daughters, that is, who were, like himself, from families that had something to do with the college. In fact, it was open to anyone at all who could pay the quite modest fees. At Medary, everybody was known by his or her first name. But at John Dewey kids were known by their surnames, as they would have been at Eton or Harrow in the U.K. This was why, though he was "Westy" at home and among his very few close friends, he thought of himself from very early on as "Westmont." And nobody ever called him Timothy.

When the bus pulled out of the church parking lot, Westmont thought he'd better begin doing something to occupy himself during the two-hour drive to Tar Hollow Camp. As he leaned over to pull some pamphlets on the Ohio Hocking Hills out of his duffle bag, he heard a girl's voice saying very close to his ear, "Isn't your name Timothy?" He looked up in surprise and saw he was being addressed by the person sitting directly across the aisle from him. She had a bright smile and was very pretty. Also, he noticed at once, she had breasts. Not all the girls in Westmont's church or school groups did. Moreover, she had on a very tight sweater and, as he would have known later, the kind of bra that shapes, narrows, and lifts the breasts of the newly breasted in the most fetching way possible. A thought went through his dazzled mind: She is almost a woman.

"Timothy's my real first name," he said, "but people call me Westy around home and Westmont at school.

"Westmont?" she laughed.

He blushed. "I guess it's the school tradition or something. Everyone's called by their last names, even the girls. Except for girls they tack on a Miss."

"So I'd be Miss Rollins at your school?"

"If that's your last name."

"It is. I'm Jill Rollins, and my parents know your parents, which is why I know who you are. And I've seen you a couple of times at college events for families."

"Is your dad a professor?"

"No, my mom is. My dad's a doctor."

"What's your mom teach?"

"Psychology. But she's gone off on some new thing called parapsychology, and she's also into a guy called Wilhelm Reich. She keeps joking that if she continues to follow these things up the department will give her the boot. My dad's not hot on them either and doesn't think they're scientific. He completely cracks up and rolls his eyes when she sits in her Orgone Box."

"What's that?"

"It's supposed to collect orgone energy. Stuff that's good for you. Say if you've got a sore knee and sit in there for an hour you can take the pointer hanging from a string at the top and point it at the sore place. The orgone energy makes it better. I think I ought to start reading all this camp stuff now. But I'll see you around Tar Hollow."

Westmont went back to his own pamphlets and booklets. Immediately he found things that troubled him. He had always feared what he thought of as Wild Nature, and there appeared to be plenty of that at Tar Hollow. For all its excitements his local ravine was kept up by the city. All the "nature" there was most definitely tamed by teams of workmen who arrived to mow the grass, trim the trees, and look after the creek beds and river banks. They even sprayed the place once a week for mosquitoes and other pests. You rarely got so much as a tick bite down his ravine, but here was something that immediately caught his eye about rattlesnakes. He looked over at Jill Rollins, but she was deep into her own reading now. Then he finally turned fully around to look at Buddy Dagger, who was sprawled alone in the back seat, asleep with his mouth hanging open.

He quickly returned to his pamphlets. "Tar Hollow is part of a larger protected complex surrounded by the rugged foothills of the Appalachia Plateau. Its twisting park and forest roads pass through deep ravines and dense woodlands. Scattered shortleaf and pitch pines growing on the ridges were once the source of tar for early settlers, hence the name Tar Hollow. The forest not only supports a variety of hardwoods but also contains a vast array of ferns, mosses, mushrooms and wildflowers. Bloodroot, wild geranium, cardinal flower and Solomon's Seal are typical wildflowers found in the forest." So much for flora, which all seemed benign enough, although he guessed they left out poison ivy on purpose. When he read on about the fauna—"Numerous reptiles and amphibians and secretive mammals can be found here"—he knew that what his eye had just caught before was about to reappear in full context with all those reptiles and secretive mammals. "The timber rattlesnake, dwindling in Ohio due to deforestation, holds on in Tar Hollow's forest. The skunk, the elusive fence lizard, the lumbering box turtle, salamanders, wild turkeys, grouse, and even bobcats are plentiful in this unique, wild region." There it was. And Westmont was afraid of snakes. Nor was he keen on lizards and salamanders. No one had warned him about these reptiles and "secretive mammals." Timber rattlers doubtless had a nest directly under the cabin to which he'd be assigned, with a family of bobcats living in the closet and skunks under his bed.

Stashing the pamphlet back in his duffle bag, he pulled out the paperback book his father had bought him after a visit to the college museum of natural history, Robert Silverberg's *The Mound Builders*. He opened to a random page. "De Soto would have done well to quit his journey and return to Spain to enjoy his Peruvian wealth. He would have avoided the torments of a terrible march through 350, 000 square miles of unexplored territory, and would have spared himself an early grave." Westmont stopped there. De Soto was probably bitten by a rattlesnake looking for the Lost Tribes of Israel at Mound City, or descendents of the architect of Serpent Mound. He knew the camp group would be visiting these sites. It was printed on the daily schedule for the second Tuesday. He read the first sentence of the blurb. "Mr. Silverberg describes, with gleeful and copious quotation, the early literature of speculation which attributed these monuments to Phoenicians, stray Vikings, refuges from Atlantis, an extinct race of giants, and Welshmen." He fell asleep.

Two hours later Westmont was storing his gear under his bunk in Beta cabin on the boys' hill. Once off the bus at the end of a long dirt road ending at Tar Hollow's Common Lodge, all the campers had gathered together in the dinning hall to be assigned cabins and given their initial instructions. Most of what they were told by the camp director, Mr. Atkins, repeated what Westmont had already read in the bus. Atkins especially emphasized the prohibitions against boys visiting the girls' hill under any circumstances, and the rule against swimming in the lake at times other than those scheduled in each day's program of events. While they were listening to all this, Westmont glanced at Jill Robbins, who gave him a smile and a wave. Through some exceptionally bad luck, Westmont had been assigned to the same cabin as Buddy Dagger. On the other hand, the assistant minister's son, Peter Robinson, was also among the eight boys in Beta cabin. Pete had always been kind to Westmont, though he was also a little aloof. All eight boys had trudged together up the narrow path beyond a pump outside the main building from which they first filled their canteens with water that smelled and tasted like rotten eggs. Westmont had quickly chosen a bottom bunk once they reached the cabin. Peter Robinson threw his duffle bag on the bunk above him, and Buddy Dagger flopped down on the lower bunk opposite.

"When do we raid the girls' hill?" Buddy asked.

"We don't," said Peter Robinson. "It's against the rules."

"You talk like a preacher's son," said Buddy.

"Maybe that's because I *am* a preacher's son."

Buddy was quiet for a moment as everyone continued organizing their gear and making up their beds. Then he said, "Anybody bring a gun?"

"Come on, Dagger," said Peter Robinson.

"You think I'm shittin' you," said Buddy. "I'll bet you Westy Westmont brought a gun. Hey Westy, you bring a gun?"

"Of course not," Westmont said.

"Of course not, of course not," mocked Buddy Dagger.

Peter Robinson said: "They let us make sling shots in woodworking class. You go out and find a Y-shaped stick, tie on thick rubber bands, and attach a leather pouch for the stone. If you find a good and strong stick to begin with, it's really neat."

"Oh, neat!" said Buddy.

Westmont said, "Kind of like Tom Sawyer."

"Who's Tom Sawyer?" Buddy asked.

"The hero of a book," said Peter Robinson.

"What book is that?" asked Buddy.

"*Tom Sawyer*," Westmont said. "By Mark Twain."

Buddy said, "You'd know Westy Westmont would read some book. Or maybe it was read to him at bedtime by his mother. Westy likes a story before bed. A couple of years ago I'd always see him in his room when I was in my tree fort, pulling up the covers, and his mother sitting there beside him in a chair reading some stupid story book. It happened every night. She still tells him to come home before the streetlights come on. Everybody in the neighborhood knows he's a sissy. Most of the fun in our neighborhood happens after it gets dark. He thinks he's cool because his dad's a so-called professor. He's afraid of Glen Echo Alley. Ask him why he won't walk down it any more."

"Leave him alone," said Peter Robinson. "We'll all make slingshots tomorrow. That'll be a good time."

Buddy Dagger said, "We can shoot stones at all the little kids in cabin Alpha Minus higher up the boys' hill. But that's just for practice. Before we raid the girls' hill."

When everyone had settled into the cabin, the eight boys sat around for a while on their bunks without talking. Most were going over the lists of the next day's events they had been given, and making sure their kits, canteens, lunch boxes, Bibles, pocketknives, flashlights, and other necessities were in good order. The flashlights were important because the trails up to the cabins were pitch dark all the way from the water pump to the highest point on the hill, which had a single light post with a flickering fluorescent bulb that attracted every kind of insect. No one could figure out why it was there at all, since it was about three hundred yards beyond the highest cabin and stood absolutely alone among the tallest trees. Eventually, one by one or in pairs, the boys started down the hill to dinner. Only Buddy Dagger hung back, saying he'd be along in a while. Westmont and Peter Robinson walked together, Peter pointing out various things to be careful of—poison ivy, big roots that could catch your toe if you ran down the hill, places where large animals or snakes had been seen—as they headed for the main lodge. Since Beta cabin was the second highest on the boys' hill, it was about a fifteen minute walk.

At dinner, Westmont caught another look at Jill Rollins. She saw that he was looking at her and gave him her little wave and a smile. She was three tables away, but he could see when she leaned over to say something to the girl sitting beside her and when the two of them looked over at him together. Westmont looked down at his plate. Everyone at his table was hungrily twirling spaghetti on their forks and spraying the tomato sauce all over each other in the process. They drank Cool Aid from the large pitchers in the middle of the table, and some of the boys poured it not only in their plastic glasses but also into their canteens for later on. It tasted better than the sulfa water that came out of the pump, though the Cool Aid powder was presumably mixed with the same wretched stuff. Everyone had been warned to be sure to have a full canteen of water once they went up the hill for the night. There was no running water near the cabins. If you got thirsty in the night and didn't have something in your canteen you would have to go all the way down the hill again to the pump. Only toward the end of dinner did Buddy Dagger arrive at the table, eating quickly and greedily in silence.

Following dinner there was some singing in the hall, and then everyone walked down to the lake to watch the sun set over the water and drop below the high hills. A swimming area had been formed with a long dock in the shape of an upside down L. Many of the boards were coming loose, and the half-exposed nails looked dangerous for people walking barefoot. There was a low diving board and a ten-foot diving board, both of them really just planks of wood with very little spring to them. The shoreline was dense with tall grass, pussy willows, and milkweed. Lots of turtles could be seen on the trunks of fallen trees. The fishing was said to be good. The main point of walking down to the lake was to hear the waterfront director give a talk on swimming safety. The water was said to be surprisingly cold for that time of year, and everyone was warned that the lake was deep, even in the swimming area. No one was to swim on the far side of the docks under any circumstances. Also, wading along the shoreline was not recommended because of the snapping turtles and biting insects in the shallows.

As the sun set behind the hills, Mr. Atkins read out the next day's schedule and said a prayer. A few of the campers took snapshots with their cameras. Between that moment and lights out was to be free time, so the campers fell into groups and pairs around the swimming area or slowly headed back to the main building. Westmont saw Jill Rollins taking off her shoes. She rolled up the bottoms of her jeans and sat down on the dock with her feet in the water. Westmont decided to join her.

"Why don't you put your feet in?" asked Jill. "It's not as cold as he said."

Westmont grinned and started taking off his socks and shoes. "It's a nice lake," he said. "It's even better than the pictures I've seen." He rolled up his own jeans and sat down on the dock beside Jill, slowly submerging his feet in the lake. He thought the water was very cold indeed. "Have you been here before?" he asked.

"You mean here at Tar Hollow Camp?"

"Yes."

"I was at camp last year, and I liked it. So I've come back."

"I suppose you know lots of the other kids, then."

"Not really. Just a couple, and they're both too religious for me."

"Aren't you religious?"

"No," she said thoughtfully, "I wouldn't really call myself religious. I come for all the fun and games and pretty much ignore the propaganda."

"Propaganda?"

"You know, all the Christian stuff."

"Oh, sure," said Westmont.

"My family doesn't go to any particular church. We used to be Unitarians, but my dad stopped going years ago and then finally my mom did too. I sure wasn't going to go on attending church by myself. I suppose you go to Main Street Presbyterian. They don't get all the campers they need from their own members, so they invite us heathens to swell the ranks. I like the sports and all the historical stuff—Mound City and all that."

"I've read a lot about the Mound Builders," Westmont said.

Out of the blue Jill Rollins suddenly changed the subject. "You know," she said. "We could come down here at night and go skinny dipping. I did that last year with a boy from North High School and we had a great time. There was a big moon and we had the lake to ourselves."

Westmont wasn't sure he knew what "skinny dipping" was, so he asked: "You mean swimming just in your skin."

"That's it," laughed Jill Rollins. "No bathing suits allowed. My parents do it together all the time, and sometimes I join in."

"You mean here at Tar Hollow?"

"No, silly. They're too old for camp. They swim a lot in our pool at home."

"You've got a home swimming pool?"

"My parents believe in getting a lot of exercise, and swimming's the best exercise there is. At least that's what my dad says."

"But we're not supposed to swim at the lake except at the posted hours."

"I know," said Jill. "But nobody really finds out if you do."

Suddenly there was a loud splash in the water. Buddy Dagger had jumped off the ten-foot board. While no one was looking, he had taken off his T-shirt and sneakers, climbed up the ladder, and done a "cannon ball," splashing everyone on the dock. Then he swam to the middle of the lake, and disappeared from the surface. He was under water for what seemed a long time, and when he reappeared, gasping for breath, his head and shoulders were covered with weeds he had pulled from deep in the lake and draped over himself. Coughing, he shouted out: "I'm the Creature from the Black Lagoon," and then dove back under the surface. When he emerged the second time, the waterfront director was holding out a long bamboo pole.

"Come on, Dagger," he said. "Take hold of this."

"I don't need it," Buddy said. He was a strong swimmer and, in spite of being breathless, swam quickly to the dock and climbed up the wooden stairs.

"That's two demerits," said the waterfront director. "You'll have to report to Mr. Atkins tomorrow morning at 9:00. And you'll forgo your scheduled swimming time tomorrow."

Jill Rollins was laughing. She turned to Westmont and said: "Impressive."

Following the events at the lake, Westmont told Jill that he'd better catch up with Peter Robinson and some others who had started back to the main building. He had been embarrassed by the talk of "skinny dipping" and annoyed by Buddy Dagger's display and disrespect for the camp rules. Westmont was wondering, given Jill's evident sophistication and physical development, if she wasn't older than she said she was, which was fifteen, only a year older than he was. It made him feel even more awkward than he usually did, but she seemed to enjoy his company. As he walked along the path past the flagpole, he looked back to see her now busy with a group of girls who were picking flowers. When he got to the lodge, he found Peter Robinson tossing a football with some boys from other cabins, and he joined in their game. Slowly the darkness came on and the boys, turning on their flashlights, headed up the hill. He and Peter walked together, talking about Buddy Dagger having gotten himself two demerits even before the first full day of camp had concluded.

"He's really a jerk, isn't he?" said Peter.

"I didn't think he'd be here," Westmont said. "I wonder how he found out about Tar Hollow in the first place."

When they reached their cabin, Westmont quickly got undressed and got into his pajamas. Across from him, Buddy was whittling at a piece of wood with his pocket knife. He didn't speak to anyone, just went on whittling, as the other five boys came in following Peter Robinson and Westmont. Westmont turned out his flashlight and slid his feet under the blankets. Buddy started to snicker even before Westmont realized he'd been "short sheeted." His feet got stuck halfway down the bed where the upper sheet had been folded back and tucked tightly under the mattress. Worse than that, Westmont's feet encountered some nasty things that had been put in the crease—dirt, pebbles, weeds, and something alive that was wriggling. Refusing to give Buddy the satisfaction of a reaction, he quietly pulled the sheet out and brushed the debris onto the floor, noting in the process that it included a collection of spiders, thousand-legged worms, and a lizard. Pretending that he had simply decided to sleep without the top sheet, he shook it out, folded it up, and put it under his bed. He thought he might talk to Mr. Atkins about changing cabins the next day.

However, things moved so swiftly the next day that Westmont never got around to asking for an appointment with Mr. Atkins. At breakfast, the camp "newspaper" was passed out to everyone. The six mimeographed sheets contained articles by the heads of each major department—ministry, athletics, and housekeeping—along with information about the local historical sites, the names and traditions of the different hills, and another list of rules and regulations. Along with all this appeared a "Tar Hollow Gossip" column written by one of the girl campers. Right at the top, in boldface, was printed:

Timothy Westmont, Timothy Westmont, How's Jill?

Westmont had barely had time to sit down before several of the breakfasting campers thrust copies of the paper at him saying, "What's this all about?" and "Who's this Jill?" and "Are you Timothy Westmont?" From that moment on he was indeed "Timothy," and no longer "Westy" Westmont to everyone at the camp except for Buddy Dagger. Although he couldn't figure out why or even when this shouting headline had been written, he did recognize the name of the "Tar Hollow Gossip" author, Maggie Andrews, who was not only a member of his church but also attended the John Dewey School. Maggie was someone who always talked about "girlfriends" and "boyfriends," and from an early age had tried to pair people up. Westmont was briefly upset by this unexpected journalistic attention, but soon enough began to realize that it might confer some status upon him. Campers looked at him, and then over at Jill Rollins. Not knowing quite what to do, Westmont quickly finished his breakfast and left the table for the bathroom. Throwing some cold water in his face, he looked at himself in the mirror. He wondered if he might be considered handsome. He had carefully combed black hair, not the crew cut or "flat-top" most common with boys his age, and, unlike many of his contemporaries, he didn't have a bad complexion. He thought he was probably too thin, but that was much better than being too fat, like Peter Robinson. He had hazel eyes with bold eyebrows, and he had begun to shave quite early. Late in the day, he even had something like an "afternoon shadow." His teeth were straight, and he had never required the expensive braces of many boys and most of the girls in his class at John Dewey. Although he didn't know the word, he thought he might possess something like virility. He left the bathroom with a confident, tall stride.

He went straight to the woodworking class, which was right on the extended and screened side porch of the main lodge. Jill and the other girls weren't attending this class as it was assumed to be something that only the boys would be interested in. All of the girls were assigned a class in spinning (on the camp's antique spinning wheels), knitting, and sewing. Boys and girls would get together once again at the Bible class, just before lunch. In woodworking, the boys were indeed allowed to make slingshots; Peter Robinson had been right about that. There were other options—birdhouses, keepsake boxes—but nearly everyone wanted to make a slingshot. The boys scouted the nearby underbrush for fallen Y-shaped sticks, bringing them up to the woodwork instructor for approval. If the wood was hard enough, and the shape would allow a small stone to pass through the Y in its pouch, the stick was approved and the work of peeling away the bark and carving a distinctive design into the handle began. After that, two bands of strong rubber were tied to the upright sides, a leather pouch cut out and attached, and the contraption was tested with pebbles collected in advance by the instructor. Rules, of course, were set down at once—chiefly that no one was to shoot a stone at another person under any circumstances. An old target saved from an earlier camp's archery class served as the object of practice. Once the slingshot was made and approved, a boy could practice aiming and shooting at the target. Very quickly Peter Robinson, Westmont, and Buddy Dagger completed their work. While Peter and Westmont headed for the firing line twenty-five yards from the target, Buddy Dagger headed out of the screened porch and into the woods. The woodwork instructor asked him where he was going. "Hunting," said Buddy, and disappeared into the high grass and then the trees.

During the hour or so it had taken to make the slingshots, Buddy had seemed unusually quiet—quiet and sullen. He made no remarks about Westmont, and didn't join in when some of the others teased him about the "How's Jill" headline in the Tar Hollow Gossip Column. Even Peter Robinson kidded him about that. But Westmont was proud of the notoriety. The more the others teased, the more he enjoyed it. He felt certain that all of them would like to have had their names linked with Jill Rollins, and that they were envious. Nothing like this had ever happened to him before.

Jill herself was there at Bible class. Everyone was meant to have brought his or her Bible down in their knapsack at breakfast time, so there was no need to climb back up to cabins on the hills and return. Westmont, of course, had his elegant *Westminster Study Edition*. Most of the others had beat-up copies of traveling bibles that Westmont's father called "stolen Gideons." Mr. Atkins, who himself led the Bible class, noticed Westmont's bible at once. "Now here's a serious student of the Holy Word," he said in a kind of joking way.

"May I show this to the others?" he asked.

"Sure," Westmont said.

"Boys and girls," said Mr. Atkins. "This is no ordinary Bible. This is the *Westminster Study Edition*, the very edition I used in my first theology classes when I was at the seminary. It's a serious edition of the world's most serious book. It's a great edition, a classic, and something a person might be proud to own. I don't know how Timothy Westmont came to own it, but we can honor him for having it and bringing it to our camp. Timothy is clearly a scholar in the making. It takes some patience, boys and girls, to pursue the great texts in terms of their various translations and the hundreds of years of contentious interpretation of their meaning. This edition does that, and anyone who studies it will be a better person for the effort." He handed the Bible back to Westmont. He blathered on in the same manner about how blessed they all were to be together under the protection of Jesus Christ and his father in heaven. Then he turned to the passage he intended to interpret. Westmont was by then aware that Jill Rollins had come up to sit beside him.

"Wow," she whispered in his ear. "We'd all better get us one of those"—pointing to his Bible. "You've got Mr. Atkins in the palm of your hand."

Westmont was blushing. "Where's your own bible?" he whispered.

"Oh," she said. "I haven't got one. I already told you I don't believe much of that stuff. Ever seen *Porgy and Bess*? You know, 'It ain't necessarily so'?"

"What's not?"

"What Sportin' Life says: 'The things that you're liable to read in the Bible / They ain't necessarily so.'"

Somebody sitting nearby said "Shhhhhh" and so they shushed. Westmont looked around at the "stolen Gideons" on other people's laps. No one seemed to have opened them yet. He was a little shocked at what Jill had said, and sufficiently preoccupied that he wasn't attending to Mr. Atkins, who was by now incanting, almost singing a passage from Isaiah. Westmont blinked, and started to pay attention…

…and the mean man boweth down,
And the great man humbleth himself…
And he shall be brought low
And upon the cedars of Lebanon,
That are high and lifted up,
And upon the oaks of Bashan
And upon all the high mountains,
And upon the hills that are lifted up…

Westmont was quite lost, and thumbing quickly through Isaiah looking for the passage when Mr. Atkins said: "Timothy, I'll bet you've got a good footnote on what I just read. It's 2:9-17. What does your edition tell us?"

Westmont found his place and read: "All things in which men might place their trust, whether the world of nature, military fortifications, or commercial success, will be brought low. This verse, which is not in the Greek translation, was added by a later writer." Westmont looked up, perplexed.

"Well," laughed Mr. Atkins, "We don't need to worry about that last bit on translations for the moment. But you all get the point. Here we are among these ancient and beautiful hills, with trees like the oaks of Bashan and the cedars of Lebanon, and while we know they manifest the greatness of God, we also know that God will bring them low in the last days when, as Isaiah says at the beginning of Book 2, 'the mountain of the Lord's house shall be established in the top of the mountains.' That's why we have our famous Bonfire Night here at Tar Hollow on the highest of our hills, the one we call Mt. Bonfire. It's on that night, when we all dedicate our lives to something higher than ourselves and our personal wishes and ambitions, that we try to imagine an even higher mount, the very top of the mountains where the Lord's house shall be established. So keep all that in your minds, boys and girls, as we continue through our days and nights at camp. Try to keep everything in perspective. Have a great time, but also have in mind that highest hill."

Mr. Atkins stopped abruptly. He took out his handkerchief and wiped his brow. It was getting hot.

Someone in the back shouted out: "Who was that later writer who wasn't Isaiah the Greek?" It was Buddy Dagger speaking.

"That's a complicated question," Mr. Atkins said. "It's the reason the scholars have edited books like the one Timothy Westmont has. That footnote talks about a Greek translation; it doesn't imply that Isaiah was a Greek. Isaiah was a Hebrew prophet."

"That's a Jew, right?" said Buddy Dagger.

"Well, yes," said Mr. Atkins.

"Thought so," Buddy Dagger said, and slammed his Bible shut.

"You have to understand," Mr. Atkins began, "that what we Christians call the Old Testament…" But then he stopped. "It's complicated," he said, "and we should leave all that for another time. Everybody get along now to the next class, and don't forget to write that required letter to your parents. Mail collection will be at dinner tonight. Have a great day."

A few hours later, during "quiet hour," Westmont wrote to his parents.

Dear Mother and Father,

We're suppose to write you letters, so here one is. It's nicer here than I thought it was going to be. There's a beautiful lake, and some great hills and footpaths. The cabins are up on the hills—girls on one hill, boys on another. The highest hill of them all is called Mt. Bonfire, since that's where a special Bonfire Night happens every session and it seems to be the Big Religious Event. I've met a nice girl called Jill Robbins. I guess you know her parents. Anyway, she said so and said she'd seen me around and seemed to know who I was soon as I got on the bus. Problem is that Buddy Dagger's here too. The bully who lives down Glen Echo Alley. He even ended up in my cabin. He short-sheeted me the very first night. He's kind of calmed down now, but I wonder how he got accepted for the camp in the first place. I'll write again in two days. Look after the ravine.

Your son, Timothy (Westy).

P.S. That's because they call me Timothy here.

As Westmont adjusted to the camp routine, the days began to pass in a predictable way, with meals, classes, field sports, nature hikes, swimming periods, and the like. He was becoming a pretty good swimmer because he worked at it hard. No natural athlete, he was nonetheless determined to hold his own in water polo, free-style relay races, and even the butterfly, a stroke he found especially difficult. His chief motivation was the fact that Jill Rollins had her swimming period at the same time he did. Luckily, Buddy Dagger's was at another time. Without Buddy around, Westmont managed to feel relaxed. He was not all of the time under Buddy's antagonistic observation, only the occasional glances (he didn't fail to notice) of Jill Rollins. He even began to show off a bit, doing a backwards dive off the low board. Jill spent a lot of time sunning herself on the dock when the instructional part of the swimming period was over and they had a half-hour of free time. She would slip the shoulder straps of her bathing suit off her shoulders (a one piece suit, no girls her age had bikinis in those days), and hold the top up with her left hand as she settled into various positions to catch the sun. She would lie for a while on her back, then on her stomach, then on her side, each time holding the bathing suit top with a hand. From the water, Westmont watched these shiftings about with great interest. He looked like a frog, peeping above the surface at an insect he hoped soon to ingest. He was getting particularly good at treading water.

Jill Rollins was also with Westmont's group on trips to prehistoric sites. When they got on the church bus for their trip to Mound City, she sat down beside him without seeming to do anything unusual. (No other girls sat with boys.) She had her printouts and pamphlets in her lap, and Westmont had his copy of Silverberg's *The Mound Builders*. The instructor of "Prehistorical Sites," Miss Daley, a docent from the Ohio Historical Society museum in Columbus, sat directly in front of them. She was a keen teacher and conversationalist. She turned around in her seat and began talking to Jill and Westmont even before the bus was out of the parking lot.

"You know," she said, "what we're going to see isn't a Mound Builder's site. Most kids think it is. There's stuff from nearby sites that really does go that far back, Hopewell sites, stuff we've got in cabinets in Columbus. You've probably come to our museum on school trips. Gives some kids the creeps, and I admit it's spooky. Bones and skulls going back to over 1,000 BC. Antler headdress. Just the big-shots were entombed; One Hopewell skull we've got has a copper nose, would you believe it? One grave had 12,000 pearls, meteoric iron, even little sheets of hammered gold. Mica bird claws, effigy pipes like you never imagined—owls, frogs, goosenecks—all this stuff piled up like inside some Egyptian pyramid. Bear's teeth, panther teeth, terra-cotta rings. They'd put it all in the funeral house, then *poof*, they'd burn it down. Carry in the dirt and build the mound above the glowing coals. Are you two boyfriend and girlfriend?"

The question came so suddenly that neither Jill nor Westmont got it.

"What?" they asked together.

"You know, girlfriend and boyfriend."

"We just met the other day," said Westmont.

"Oh," said the docent, "sorry I asked. Just wondered. Anyway, the Serpent Mound isn't Hopewell. People think it is. Then they thought Adena, but the radiocarbon dating puts it right at A.D. 1000 or so, Fort Ancient culture. And nothing buried in it either. Absolutely beautiful, though. You can see the whole shape of it from the tower they built at one end. How did they ever do it, that's what I wonder. No bulldozers, no heavy equipment of any kind. Lots of push and shove, I guess. They built it on some rock formations no one understands. Million years ago, some asteroid, volcano, some explosion anyway, it tossed up rock 1000 feet above the ground. Clearly those Fort Ancients liked the site because it was then already risen, although settled some from all those years before. The serpent's more than a quarter mile from nose to tail. Perfectly symmetrical shaping of the undulations. Ward Putnam saved it from the farmers when he bought the place for Peabody at Harvard. Good thing, too. Imagine plowing all this down. Some say it's still got spirits lingering. Does the thing have a frog in its mouth or an egg? People disagree. 1,350 feet, to be exact, of snake. Are you two going steady?"

This time Jill Rollins spoke. "The girls in my cabin say we'd make a nice couple, but like Timothy says, we only just met."

Timothy said, "I'm just fourteen."

And Jill said, "But I'm fifteen."

By this time they had reached the site of Serpent Mound.

The tour of the mound and surrounding antiquities was uneventful. Miss Daley led the group around, saying much the same thing she had already told Jill and Westmont on the bus. The two of them walked together. For the first time, Jill mentioned Buddy Dagger.

"You really hate Buddy Dagger, don't you?" she said.

"He hates me," said Westmont.

"We've got lots of kids like him at our school," said Jill. "He's just a little rough around the edges. He could use a few hours sitting in our box."

"In your box?" asked Westmont.

"You know, I told you. My mom's Orgone box. We all use it now and then, and sometimes friends come over. You could use it too."

"I don't know quite what I'd use it for," he said.

"It's good for what ails you. Or so my mother says."

Miss Daley was making her distinctions among the Adena and Hopewell peoples, and the Fort Ancients. No one seemed to pay much attention. Several who had come on the bus seemed in fact to have wondered off to look at things in the small museum that had been built near the serpent mound. Miss Daley was saying that Harvard had turned the site over to the Ohio Archaeological and Historical Society in 1900.

"And this doctor who recommends using this box?" asked Westmont.

"Reich," she said. "He was a disciple of Freud, but broke away, like Jung."

"And why was that?" asked Westmont, who had never heard of Freud or Jung.

"You really want to know?"

"Sure."

"Well," she said, "he had some controversial ideas about sex."

"But what's that got to do with the your box?"

Before she could answer, Peter Robinson, who ran up and said he had found a carved flint, interrupted their conversation. He was trying to figure out whether it was an arrowhead or a knife blade when someone else in the group arrived to say he thought it was fake, some kind of toy dropped there by tourists like themselves who had bought it at a souvenir shop. Flints like the one Peter had found were ground out by the hundreds on a machine. He'd seen it done. He claimed that the people who bought these things were taken in by men who ran the souvenir business, and ought to save their money. Peter said he'd show the flint to Miss Daley, and ran off with his skeptical friend trotting behind. The conversation between Jill and Westmont had pretty much been ruined. Jill grinned and shrugged her shoulders. Then they, too, walked back to the group around Miss Daley.

In the days that followed the bus trip to Mound City and surrounding prehistoric sites, Buddy Dagger had become more obnoxious at night than usual. It all got especially disgusting on the third night of the camp's second week. Once all the flashlights had been turned out and the six boys in Westmont's cabin were in bed, Buddy insisted they should all tell "dirty jokes." Peter Robinson was against this, and reminded everyone they were at a church camp after all. Well, Buddy said, they didn't all have to tell jokes, some could just tell "dirty stories" instead. Peter Robinson said he didn't really see the difference.

Buddy asked if anyone among them had seen a girl's pussy. There was silence. He said he'd seen his sister's and his sister's friend's when they danced naked in the garage under his house. He said the friend had lots of pubic hair but his sister didn't. He said they both let boys from the neighborhood stick their fingers in for fifty cents.

"That's gross," said one of the boys, turning on his flashlight and shining it at Buddy's face.

"Turn it off," said Buddy. "I won't tell you any more unless it's dark."

The light went out.

Buddy said his sister had these little tits. She'd put lipstick on them and for just another fifty cents she'd let you suck them till your mouth was red. He laughed. He said he even did that with his sister himself, but not the other thing. Sometimes, he said, his sister and her friend let grown men fuck them for a few dollars each. He'd seen it through a crack in the wall.

"Other times," he said, "I've watched them with each other. They get down on the old mattress in the garage and look like they're screwing each other, even though neither one of them has a dick. It's weird."

He paused for a moment, then said it was someone else's turn.

114

No one spoke.

Well, he said, he'd have to think up a dirty joke. "One day Westy Westmont went out swimming in the lake with Jill Rollins. Westy had this big hard dick just from looking at her in her bathing suit, but then she took it off, and Wow…"

"Shut up, Buddy," Westmont said.

"And Jill was really stacked. She was just fifteen but she looked like eighteen, really big boobs. She had a big bush too, so thick you couldn't see her crack."

"Shut up, Buddy," said Peter Robinson.

Buddy stopped talking. A couple of the boys turned their flashlights on him. He raised his middle finger, made a funny shaking motion with his head.

"And what do you think happens next? What does Westy Westmont do?"

What Westmont had done by that point was to grab his flashlight, get out of bed, and start running down the trail to the main lodge still in his pajamas. *Wrong, wrong,* he thought as he ran. For Buddy to say those things that he saw. To say that about Jill Rollins. He stumbled over protruding roots on the trail and nearly fell. The beam of his flashlight picked out things in the woods that weren't really there—animals and lurking strangers emerging from behind trees. Strange phrases surfaced in his mind as he ran, beginning with something from a cowboy movie they'd been shown in the lodge a few nights before: *Get out of town, Buddy, or you're going to regret it.* Everyone from his cabin but Dagger had snickered at that. And things Jill had said all mixed up with silly Miss Daley and memories from home: Orgone box and swimming with her parents in their pool and Hopewell or Adena burial rites and then his cousin Robert saying about their games and costumes in Glen Echo *maybe we're too old for this.* And from that passage he'd been going back to in his concordance ever since his father had made him look it up: *To him that did the wrong I cry out of wrong Friend I owe them no wrong Why do ye not take wrong If he hath wronged thee what of wrath?* Wrath: *Let not the sun go down on your wrath.* But the sun had gone down and the night was dark. He slipped and sprawled on the path, skinning his elbows and knees. He got up, limping and skipping into the right pace and rhythm, familiar now from so many treks down the boys' hill. He had almost reached the bottom. When he got to the pump, he jerked the handle up and down, drank deeply of the nasty water, washed his face. Then he walked to the door of Mr. Atkins' apartment in the main lodge and, pounding on it, woke him up.

Mr. Atkins was more amused than upset when he listened to Westmont's complaints. Westmont didn't repeat Buddy's actual words—he couldn't have managed that at all—but just told him about "dirty jokes" and "dirty stories." He also said that Buddy had said some wrongful things about a girl at the camp, not naming names. Mr. Atkins had raised his eyebrows when Westmont used the word "wrongful." When Westmont said he wanted to telephone his parents, Mr. Atkins reminded him that it was the middle of the night, and anyway there was a camp rule about phone calls to campers' parents. Only letters allowed. Then he said something surprising. "You know, this Tar Hollow experience is just the kind of thing that ought to help straighten out someone like Buddy Dagger. I doubt you understand all his problems and the hardships of his family life. He has a difficult time of it in Columbus. In fact, someone like you might be in a position to help him out." Westmont stared at Mr. Atkins as if he had suddenly lost his mind.

"I don't want to help him out," Westmont said. "I just want him to leave me alone. If he doesn't, I want to go home."

Mr. Atkins suggested that Westmont should curl up on the sofa near the fireplace for the rest of the night. He felt certain that things would look better in the morning. He gave Westmont a pat on the shoulder and went back to his own bed, saying as he did so, "You're a good kid, Timothy. I bet you'll really make something of your life."

At the first sign of sunrise, Westmont crept up the path to his cabin still wearing his pajamas but with Mr. Atkins' raincoat over his shoulders. He had simply taken the raincoat when he saw it lying over a chair. He doubted that anyone would yet be awake on the boys' hill, but he didn't want someone to see him looking ridiculous. He'd return the raincoat later in the day.

The morning was clear—no need, certainly, for what he was wearing—and Westmont heard all the birds waking up. He could identify only his favorites, the cardinals and finches, along with a woodpecker pecking away on a tree just off the path. As he approached his cabin, he saw the fluorescent light go off on the pole at the top of the hill. He guessed it was on a timer. A lizard darted down the length of a fallen limb. At first he thought no one was awake in his cabin, but Peter Robinson opened his eyes as Westmont entered and gave him a funny look as he quickly slipped into his bed.

Westmont hadn't slept at all on Mr. Atkins' sofa, so he fell asleep in his bunk almost at once and didn't stir when the others had gotten up and left for the day's activities. It was late morning by the time he suddenly jerked awake in an empty cabin. At once he took out his pen and paper to write the letter home he knew would be collected later in the day. He didn't need to say very much to his parents.

Dear Mother and Father
Please come and get me. I really don't like it here and I want to go
home. I've got a big problem with Buddy Dagger. They really ought
to have adult counselors in these cabins. Peter Robinson's supposed to
be in charge because of his dad being assistant pastor and all that,
but things are getting worse and worse.

Westmont never learned whether his parents had received his letter or not. After the events that occurred on Bonfire Night it no longer made any difference.

Tradition had it that people's lives had really been changed by the Bonfire Night experience. Having nothing at all to do with Guy Fawkes or anything British, the Tar Hollow bonfire had its origins in something that the Presbyterian ministry thought of as being native American. Over the years, the presumed Indian origins got superimposed on the anthropologists' theories about the burning of prehistoric funeral houses before the heaping up of mounds. The idea of the bonfire was some kind of hodgepodge of Indian celebration out of 1950s American Westerns seen in a million cinemas like Westmont's own Hudson Street Theater at the end of Glen Echo Alley, and a confused notion of death and rebirth through fire assumed to be the point of burning the prehistoric funeral houses before heaping earth over them in ritual burial. There was talk of both these "traditions" from the first day of every session at Tar Hollow Camp.

The bonfire was prepared days ahead of time in the "Green Cathedral" at the top of the highest of all the Hocking Hills. It was a good long walk, about a mile, from the camp's main lodge, and the walk itself was part of the general objective. Total silence was to be maintained both on the flat part of the walk and, even more important, on the trail that led up to the clearing where the Green Cathedral was. The walk didn't begin until after total darkness had fallen, which meant well after nine o'clock in midsummer. The whole ritual didn't finish until midnight. Along the way, camp officials and other adult volunteers from the church who drove in just for this night stood with candles in their hands and stern expressions on their faces. On the trail, this was all rather impressive. An adult with a candle appeared at every turn, and at some points, when the trail ran straight, a camper could see four or five adults with candles before the path curved again in a series of switchbacks.

The purpose of "Bonfire Night" was to "dedicate" one's life. Everyone was required to find a stick at some point during the walk and, once the bonfire was lighted and everyone was gathered around it in the green cathedral clearing, to take turns walking up to the fire, tossing in the stick he had chosen, and saying "I dedicate my life to…" To something. That was the hard part. The campers had been told that they should spend much of the week and a half leading up to Bonfire Night thinking about their "dedication." They weren't required—it was understood that they were unable at their age—to make a dedication that committed them for life. But they shouldn't choose something frivolous. They should perhaps think about a time-span of three or four years, and what seemed really important and worth doing during that period. And they should take their lead from the adults, who would make the first dedications. As the last of the walking campers—and they were to walk single file—passed the first candle-holding adult, the adult would himself join in the line until eventually all of the adults keeping guard along the trail had become part of the line and themselves arrived behind the campers in the green cathedral. At that point the campers would be directly in front of the bonfire and a semi-circle of adults would be standing behind them.

After Westmont sealed the letter to his parents, he remembered that Bonfire Night would be upon them that very evening. He wouldn't be able to get out of the "dedication." Thinking about what he should say, he decided that dedicating himself to Biblical study would sound suitably profound, or at least get him through the event without making things any more difficult for himself than they already were before he could get out of Tar Hollow and go home. He wanted to sound predictable and dull in order not to call any more attention to himself than circumstances already had, and everybody already knew about his famous Bible. He was pretty sure he wanted out of there as soon as possible, but also he had to admit that he'd miss doing things with Jill Rollins. Maybe he should tough it out for the remaining three days. He didn't even know where she lived in Columbus and had been trying to work up the courage to ask. He knew that in situations like these it was even okay to ask for a phone number. It also occurred to him that, once back in Columbus, he might see her at places where Buddy Dagger would never dare to show his face—at the Faculty Club, for example, where he sometimes had dinner with his parents and assumed she might, now and then, have dinner with hers. Maybe they could all have dinner together.

He passed the day in a kind of daze, waiting for the climb up to the bonfire. He skipped a few of his classes, even the Bible study class, lurking around the kitchen and talking to one of the cooks. Nor did he go swimming that day. He thought he might be getting a little sick—his ears hurt, and they'd been warned about a fungus that some swimmers picked up in the lake—and he thought his eyes looked red when he looked at himself in the main lodge mirror. He also thought his hair looked bad. It didn't matter if the boys with crew cuts and flattops washed their hair or not, but when he didn't do it, as his mother always reminded him, his longish brown hair looked greasy and unkempt. He hadn't washed his hair for days.

Eventually, following the evening meal in the dining hall and some free time in the yard directly in front, it was time to begin the march. Mr. Atkins blew a playground whistle to assemble everyone around the flagpole. Adults, both those whom he recognized and others who had just arrived, took their candles and disappeared into the distance. The campers were told to form a single-file line and stand there in silence. After a while, Mr. Atkins whispered to the camper at the head of the line to begin walking, and so they all filed along looking for a good stick to pick up along the way.

Westmont found himself walking between two boys he didn't know at all. Almost at once they both leaned down and picked up impressive-looking sticks a couple of feet long and thick in the middle. Westmont just trudged along. The walk to the trail head produced a cloud of dust, and those in the middle of the column, or toward the end, could be heard coughing. Someone shouted to the front "Don't kick up dust!" and then everyone heard Mr. Atkins shouting back, "Total silence! Total silence now!" There was grumbling in the ranks. Westmont thought he heard a boy saying something gross. He had no idea where Jill Rollins was in the file, and craned his neck around to look. The line appeared to recede into infinity behind him. His brain was playing tricks on him again: *Out of exile into promised land* repeated in his head like a sound loop. Adena folk. The Hopewells. Obsidian black and mica claw, Jeff Chandler in the movie he liked best, *Broken Arrow.* Jimmy Stewart in that too. Did they have a bonfire in that film? Did they have a dedication in a green cathedral? At the Hudson Theater they had a Roy Rogers Club on Saturdays; you could win a prize. With a really first-rate Rogers imitation you were sent to regionals and even Hollywood for finals. Peter Robinson had won a pie-eating contest at the Hudson, but that was when they were younger. Anyway he'd dedicate his life to Bible study, then get out of town. No one knew about his games in the ravine except for Buddy Dagger, or about the yellow plume in his three-cornered hat.

As they approached the beginning of the trail, Westmont saw what he thought was a suitable stick. He picked it up and began peeling off the bark as he walked. When that was done, he took out a handkerchief and rubbed the stick as if he were polishing it, somehow trying to make it fit for his offering of a dedication. He passed by the trail's first adult, standing like an austere carved figure in a medieval church, holding his candle at the height of his waist, watching the line of campers pass by with a stern expression on his face. Soon there was another candle-bearer, this time a woman with long hair, someone's mother he supposed. Between candle-bearers it was very dark, and everyone stepped carefully, only accustomed to climbing the hills at night with their flashlights on. The trail narrowed, then seemed to be wider again. A few of the campers began walking in pairs, but they were admonished by the next candle-bearer. The line again was single file, stretching as far forward and as far back as Westmont could see. Something brushed his face in the dark—a bat, he feared—but it was only some leaves on a low branch. He clutched his stick is if it were a weapon. Something was making him sweat, probably the steep climb itself, though everyone was walking slowly.

After what seemed to be an interminable length of time, the line of campers filed into a clearing at the top of the hill—the Green Cathedral— and could see a great heap of wood at the very center—the kindling, twigs and faggots waiting to be lighted at just the right moment. Westmont could see Mr. Atkins standing at a kind of rustic altar. Two candle-bearers began to form the line into an orderly semi-circle around what was about to be the fire. When the last campers in the line had joined the group in the clearing, the earliest candle-bearers, who had by then joined it, formed in their turn a second semi-circle behind the first.

"Welcome," Mr. Atkins said, "To Bonfire Night."

The candle-bearers spoke back in unison: "And Welcome to you." As a group, they extinguished their candles.

At that point Mr. Atkins lighted a torch that had been prepared with a system of ropes and pulleys to rise at first to the height of the highest tree and then descend rapidly down a wire anchored in the kindling, which had been soaked in gasoline. The torch dropped as if from the heavens and the stack of wood burst into flame. There was an intake of breath among the campers and murmurs of appreciation from the adults who had been to bonfire night before and knew in advance what would happen. The fire quickly began to consume the larger branches. It blazed brightly in the darkness.

As everyone had been prepared for these solemnities, Mr. Atkins only needed to raise and lower his arm as if he were a conductor beginning an orchestral performance for the first person to step forward and dedicate his life. Appropriately enough, this was the church choir director. He walked up to the fire, threw on his stick, and said with confidence and clarity: "I dedicate my life to the worship of God through music." Other adults separated themselves from the semicircle of candle-bearers behind the campers. Mr. Atkins had asked several of them to step up quickly in order to establish an example he hoped the campers would follow.

Up came a woman Westmont recognized from around his neighborhood. She was known to be involved with charities like "Main Street Cares" and "March of Dimes." She tossed in her stick and said: "I dedicate my life to helping the poor."

Up came a doctor who said: "I dedicate my life to healing."

And then someone who said: "I dedicate my life to being a good father."

So it went. After a while there were repetitions in the dedications, along with a lot of foolishness when people who hadn't really thought about it realized they had to walk up and say something. Peter Robinson was the first camper to walk up, and he had said: "I dedicate my life to helping out at home." *Pathetic*, thought Westmont. Certainly Peter could have done better than that. A matronly woman known to be the heart and soul of the scouting movement walked up and said, "I dedicate my life to the Girl Scouts." Another camper walked up and said, "I dedicate my life to looking after animals." It became a tedious procession. A few of the adults decided at the last moment to make a harmless joke of it, like old Mrs. McCurdy who ran the Home-Made Deli on Summit Street: "I dedicate my life to my apple pies," she said. A quiet and thoughtful man who was a church deacon said: "I dedicate my life in the privacy of my mind." Westmont was not sure when he should go forward, and was more or less waiting for another foolish-sounding dedication before following on with his own, when to his surprise Buddy Dagger strode brazenly forward looking tough and smug:

"I dedicate my life to Jill Rollins," he said. And then, as if he understood that people would find this strange or inappropriate, he said it again, a little louder:

"I dedicate my life to Jill Rollins."

There was a little tittering among the campers and adults, and then some outright laughter. Westmont felt sick. Buddy looked around him triumphantly, tossed his stick in the flames, and joined the group who had already spoken on the other side of the fire. Westmont looked around for Jill but couldn't see her. Feeling dizzy, he walked forward with his stick thinking he had better get it over with. Before he could speak, he felt what he thought was bullet hitting him under his right eye. His hand went to his cheekbone and came away covered with blood. Staggering forward, he stayed conscious just long enough to toss his stick on the fire and see Buddy Dagger on the other side with his slingshot still in his hand. He heard a kind of voice in his head like the one he had been hearing off and on all day saying, *You've got to admit he's a very good shot.* Then he fell flat on his face.

When it was realized that Westmont was actually unconscious, everything stopped. The doctor who had "dedicated his life" to healing immediately determined that the injury might be serious and discovered that the object that had hit and possibly broken Westmont's right cheekbone was in fact a steel ball bearing, later discovered to have come from a machine shop owned by Buddy Dagger's uncle. Dagger himself had disappeared into the woods. A makeshift stretcher was quickly constructed with branches and twine. As no one, not even the adults, had been allowed to bring a flashlight up to the Green Cathedral, Westmont was carried down the hill on his stretcher by candlelight by a series of teams, mostly men, but including the scout mistress and a few other strong women. No one thought about looking around for Jill Rollins. By the time the procession, looking a little like some kind of pagan funeral, reached the main lodge, Westmont was coming around, but still seemed delirious. A thermometer was found by the camp nurse, and Westmont had an alarming fever of over 103 degrees. Of course his parents were phoned at once. Making the drive to Tar Hollow in less than two hours, they still took long enough that by the time they arrived to take Westmont home every kind of rumor was circulating: Timothy and Buddy Dagger had been fighting over a girl; the girl herself wasn't a member of the church and was known to be sexually provocative on the waterfront and to have told a number of people about a box she sat in at home meant to do all kinds of strange things, including increasing libido. When Westmont's father realized that his son's cheekbone had been broken by a steel ballbearing shot from a powerful slingshot, he immediately phoned his lawyer and asked what he should do to protect

Westmont from his assailant, who in fact lived very nearby in Columbus. Within hours Buddy Dagger was found and, as he was a minor who seemed to have no parents, remanded to the Juvenile Justice Center in Columbus. There he was incarcerated pending a trial in juvenile court for "assault." Jill Rollins seemed to have vanished into thin air.

In the hours that followed his injury, Westmont was found to have not only a broken cheekbone but also pneumonia. Treated at home with what were then new antibiotics, he slowly recovered, though he lived for the rest of his life with a clearly visible dent in his face where he had been struck by the steel ball bearing. His parents, of course, were only able to read his last letter home after he was under their care, safe in his bed. Furthermore, it turned out that Westmont was unwilling to discuss the incident at all and, for that reason, Buddy Dagger was released from the Juvenile Justice Center pending Westmont's willingness, through his parents and their lawyer, to press charges. Westmont made it clear that all he wanted was for things to "get back to normal." For him, that meant above all other things, a trip in costume down the ravine. It was still, after all, late summer. When the antibiotics kicked in, and even before his cheekbone had properly begun to heal, Westmont put on his favorite costume—a Horatio Hornblower outfit—that included his three-corner hat with its yellow plume. Taking along his grandfather's Spanish American War sword, he gingerly stepped down the slippery shale on the hill and entered Glen Echo Park. He was away for some time and, of course, his parents worried about allowing their son's single-minded ritual to take place at all. But he returned by dusk, saying that now he "felt much better."

In years to come, Westmont's cousins, Robert and Richard, would say that in their view, having heard from Westmont's parents about their son's convalescent descent, "Westy never came up out of that ravine at all." There was some truth in that. Among other things, Westmont never afterwards paid much attention to Robert and Richard themselves, though his parents stayed in contact. He would say, when their names were mentioned, "Oh, all that's over now." As for Jill Rollins, he alluded to her only once, asking his father if there was a Professor Rollins in the college who had a daughter. His father said there was a Robbins, but no Rollins, at least as far as he knew. The Columbus phone book listed a Dr. Rollins, but only at an office number. When he finally gathered enough courage to phone, the secretary was put out when he asked if Dr. Rollins had a daughter. "If he does, it's none of your business," she said. Numbly, he thumbed on in the R's, calming himself by mumbling over the list: *Roloff, Rolston, Roman, Romeo, Romero, Rooney.*

Long after he had left home and acquired his academic degrees and qualifications, Westmont still wondered whatever became of the girl at Tar Hollow. In his later life, he was never very confident with women, even though he was eventually married for a short time. His awkwardness, he thought, really had begun at that camp. But there were also times when he thought that Jill Rollins might have been some kind of apparition. Otherwise, how did it happen that not a single person he knew ever mentioned her or seemed to have known her or even her name? He would occasionally laugh to himself about the Reichian Box and "Orgone Energy." As for the *Westminster Study Edition* of the Holy Bible, it was still on his shelf. Now and then, in his career as an archivist, he had occasion to consult the concordance. In the texts themselves, especially Isaiah, he was embarrassed to read his juvenile marginalia. He grew up to be one of those strange creatures that prefer books to people. It depressed him, when he let himself dwell on the fact, to acknowledge this. It's something that he might have talked over with a pretty young girl, someone like Jill.

Westmont and the Different Kinds of Music

5

It had been a very strange summer. Westmont was soon to enter graduate school to study library science. In order to pay at least some of the fees himself, he worked for the Ohio State Auditor typing audit reports on the new IBM Selectric typewriters. They were great for multiple margins, especially if you were typing figures rather than words. For a while, he got real aesthetic pleasure from typing the reports. By the end of the summer, however, the daily grind was driving him nuts. During coffee breaks he was reading poems by Wallace Stevens in Oscar Williams' *Pocket Book of Modern Verse*. He'd settled on Stevens mainly because he couldn't understand his poems at all. At one point, he typed a fragment or line of Stevens into the figures:

$2,365,748.48
$1,757,285.23
$Mother of beauty
$5,683,194.00
$On extended wings

And so on. No one ever caught him. Stevens had said, "Money is a kind of poetry." But was poetry a kind of money? The music in his head all summer long was "We Shall Overcome." He had joined CORE (Congress of Racial Equality) and had participated in a few local civil rights marches. As a result of doing this, he thought well of himself. None of his friends appeared at these demonstrations, though he persuaded his girlfriend to come along once. It was the summer of 1963. Everyone was waiting to see what would happen when the march on Washington got under way at the same time as the Ohio State Fair. Everyone, that is, involved either with the Fair itself or government offices in Columbus. Westmont had been asked by his boss, the First Assistant to Bud Tracy, Ohio State Auditor, to man the Auditor's Office exhibit at the fair. This sounded to Westmont like a good break from the figures, even a good break from Wallace Stevens. He went around humming "We Shall Overcome." Very few people remember that James Baldwin's novel, *Another Country*, was actually censored and confiscated in various cities during the summer of 1963. Westmont watched the raid on the biggest downtown bookstore in Columbus from his desk in the Auditor's office. The police actually raided the store and took out the entire inventory of Baldwin's book. Westmont was angry about this. James Baldwin wasn't Wallace Stevens, but he was Literature. When the cops had left, he took a coffee break and walked across the street to the bookstore and asked: "Can I get a copy of *Another Country*?" He could not.

A week later he drove his car to the Ohio State Fair rather than to the Auditor's parking place at the State House. As he parked the car, the radio began to broadcast Martin Luther King's "I Have a Dream" speech. He was hearing this live, and it wasn't yet a famous speech. It was happening *right now*. Westmont sat there in his car, overwhelmed. When it was over, he walked to the State Offices tent in a kind of semi-delirium, mumbling *We Shall Overcome, We Shall Overcome*. His boss said: "What's that?" and Westmont said, "A CORE button." His boss said, "Take that off and put this on." He was given a button that said "Reelect Bud Tracy." Five days later he left for Stanford University.

Westmont as Talbot Eastmore

My real name is not Timothy Westmont, it's Talbot Eastmore. I have no English wife, but because I rather wish I did, I've married Westmont to an English woman in two of the foregoing fictions. (Westmont's wife did, poor guy, leave him in actual fact and return to the UK.) This time, while writing a sixth story, I want to stick more to the truth of things. But I also want to write about a close friend who has read some of the Westmont stories—the five published here but also some others that no one will ever see—and who wouldn't want his actual name to appear in something like fiction (although this isn't fiction. I'm not sure about "like"). Anyway, I'll call him Ernest Webber, which is what he called himself now and then in certain situations and what James Walton called him in the unpublished novel now in my care. I write as if we're all still in the present, though in fact poor Webber recently died. Because it's hard for me to imagine him no longer alive, I'll probably sometimes forget to do that—write about him, that is, as someone who is no longer alive. I'll get messed up with chronology and write as if I could still drive out to his house and visit him, probably using the wrong tense sequences, too.

What a business, trying to get these things straight! In part I want to write about a friendship here, one of the great subjects of literature. Nothing like love, you'll say, but I'll say you're wrong. A great friend is as rare as a great love. As it happens, most of my close friends—strange thing, a close friend, especially after a certain age—have been more or less completely nuts except for Webber, who was completely sane. Being entirely ordinary myself, I've always looked for extraordinary friends. It's like an ugly man looking for beautiful women. "Oh, you're gay," I can hear you saying. Not a bit of it. That's the most tedious thing about readers of a literature of friendship at the present time. Everybody thinks the friends are gay—Huck and Jim, Ishmael and Queequeg. Like all the other bookish types of my generation, I read Leslie Fiedler in the 1960s, one of the people who started this craze and upset innocents like Ernest Hemingway about good friends probably being queer. I even knew Fiedler's son, by the way, who was going out with Susan Clodd at Stanford. (Think which Susan comes to mind who's not any longer called Clodd but who's a famous poet and you'll know who I mean.) But all close friends, I tell you, are not necessarily gay.

After high school, I didn't have any friends at all for a while. This is because my first great love arrived at just that point—the summer after graduation—and sucked up all the oxygen in the universe that might have sustained a friendship with someone during my undergraduate years at Ohio State. I've had three great friends and two great, but disastrous, loves. That doesn't sound like a lot of either, but it's plenty. Especially as some of the friendships and some of the loves occurred in a way that overlapped. I remember the second of my great loves asking me early in our relationship, "How many women have you slept with?" When I said, "just one," she cracked up giggling. In her case there had been—I forget the actual number—lots of men. I was at first afraid that my love-making must have suggested that my own experience was on the meager side. But, believe me, one woman was enough for those four years if it was someone like Cora. She was insatiable. She was also such a neurotic responsibility that I barely had time for my classes, let alone a serious friendship. At a huge university like OSU, one got lost in the crowd and was lucky to have anyone at all to confide in. I'd walk from class to class, building to building, always worried about Cora, and wishing I had a friend to whom I could tell my joys and woes.

A complicated part of this was that Cora opposed what I had always thought of as "the probable course of my life." I wanted to be a librarian, or at any rate to live among books. She was hoping for a calling rather more romantic. An NFL quarterback, perhaps. When we first met, I was in my Jewish phase. My one close high-school friend was a Jew, and his very impressive parents were academic. At home, I was increasingly at odds with my own family about politics, culture, education, and everything else. The first time I had dinner at Joel's house I experienced a revelation. I had never in my life been part of an intellectual conversation at table. All his parents' friends—five or six around the table with their wives (who hardly spoke)—were clearly men of genius. And of course Jews. Smart people were Jews. It had occurred to me before, but only in the abstract. My own family's friends never talked like this. They were Republicans, Presbyterians, WASPs. As it happened, I was auditing a course at OSU taught by the smartest professor in the entire world, Harvey Goldberg. We studied the Dreyfus Affair and Zola's heroic intervention. My own parents had never heard of Dreyfus or Zola. When I first met Cora, she asked me what I wanted to be, and I said "a Jew." She said, "That's the funniest thing I've ever heard."

You have to remember that this was the great moment in Jewish fiction and culture generally. Bernard Malamud had prepared the way for Bellow and Roth and even Cleveland's own Herbert Gold. Everyone would soon be going to Woody Allen movies. Historians were beginning to realize that most of the "original thought" in America wasn't properly "American" at all, but the contribution of Jews who had fled from Europe before or during the Second World War and ended up on one coast or another to do their work. Three of the men around that dinner table at Joel's house fell into this category. Two of them were artists, like Joel's father, and the third, who had come from Vienna and had actually known Schoenberg and Wittgenstein, was a historian who was a colleague of Harvey Goldberg's. I had never heard of Schoenberg or Wittgenstein, but I sat at Goldberg's feet three times a week and thought he was the smartest person I'd ever known. Given the amazing electronic developments that have occurred in recent years, you can actually hear snippets from his eloquent lectures of nearly a half-century back by "visiting" a website: HG Center, Madison: http://history.wisc.edu/goldberg/goldberg.htm. Give it a try before reading on. You'll be enlightened and impressed.

Cora, like her parents, was an Episcopalian. When she first let me put my hand on her breasts, she said—"This Jewish thing, you're kidding, right? These are Episcopalian tits." When I lied and said I was kidding, she also let me put my hand in her pants, but the long-term problem that we had eventually to resolve turned out to be that I really did want to become a Jew. It was even worse, from Cora's point of view, that I also wanted to be an archivist. She'd say, gazing at me in wonder or contempt (it was hard to tell): "A Jewish librarian. What you want out of life is to be a Jewish librarian." She claimed that both Jews and librarians were afraid of sex. I asked her how she knew. She said this was something that was "generally understood." "By Episcopalians?" I asked. "By everyone," she said. The weirdest thing about our relationship was that she was still in high school. One year younger than I was, she attended Upper Arlington High. I had recently moved to the Upper Arlington part of Columbus myself, but always attended the University School, a John Deweyite progressive education proudly part of my dossier and something that all my Jewish friends understood and approved of. The school was run by the OSU education department as a "laboratory" for educational experiments. One of the experiments was to allow seniors to take classes at OSU, which is how I had met Harvey Goldberg.

Harvey had written a biography of the great French Socialist and orator Jean Jaurès. Reviewers said that it read like a Balzac novel. Since Balzac, even before Zola, was one of my early heroes, I thought if a biography read like his kind of novel I'd probably like it. I read it soon after it was published and was converted to Socialism in a flash. Cora said, "So now you're a Jewish Socialist Librarian. I'm really a lucky girl." What she didn't know was that Harvey was acquainted with the OSU archivist, an actual, living Jewish Socialist Librarian. I had explained about Cora's lack of enthusiasm for my calling during a long lunch with Harvey. He said, "Have you ever been up to The Cage?" I said I wasn't sure what he meant. "Banned book collection," said Harvey. "Banned images as well. I'll write you a note to Joshua Solomon giving you access to the restricted collection on the grounds that you're a serious student interested in contemporary fiction. I'll say you need to read Henry Miller's *The Tropic of Cancer*, which they've got up there along with his other books. Miller's really very good. Take your girlfriend along. She may get something of a shock, but she'll probably like what she sees. And she'll have a new idea about what archives are all about, and maybe a little respect for the people who run them." So a few days later I picked up Cora outside Upper Arlington High in my Studebaker Lark. "Let's go get some pizza and a beer," she said. I said with determination, "In fact we're going to the OSU library." "Oh, no!" she said. "Oh yes," I replied. "We're going to check out Henry Miller in the collection of banned books."

You have to understand that this was 1959. You could buy *Ulysses* even as a Modern Library book, though it was still considered prudent to preface that edition with Judge John M. Woolsey's opinion of December 6, 1933, which lifted the ban. Miller was still beyond the pale. So was *Lady Chatterley*. Something like *The Story of O* was still unthinkable. It amazes me that kids these days flip on their laptops and watch every kind of screwing ever dreamed of on their screens while "multi-tasking" at their homework and text-messaging their friends at the same time.

"I hope this is good," said Cora, as we took the elevator up to the seventh floor.

"It's part of our education," I said seriously. "And it's a glimpse of how I intend to lead my life." (Not living like Henry Miller, of course, but like the dusty, stooped man who unlocked the door to a windowless room containing not only all of the works of Mr. Miller, but, A to Z, floor to ceiling, the pornography of the ages.) Mr. Solomon asked if I had a note from my professor. I showed him Harvey's letter, and he laughed. "You know Harvey Goldberg, then?" I told him I was auditing his French history class. "Lucky you," said Mr. Solomon, "Harvey's one of the best. You understand, don't you, that I'll have to lock you in. This is a restricted area. When you're ready to leave, just push this button that looks like a doorbell. It rings right at my desk."

Cora, looking around, was getting interested. "Oh," she said, "You've got dirty pictures as well as dirty books."

"The whole tradition," said Mr. Solomon. "Even some old blue movies."

"Blue movies?" She asked.

"Yes," he said.

"What's this?" she asked, picking up what looked like a large black and white drawing.

"A Beardsley print," Solomon, said. "I've got a scholar up from the Kinsey Institute working on quality erotic images."

"The Kinsey Institute?"

"At I.U. in Bloomington. This is an Aubrey Beardsley print," he said. "It's an extremely fine example of a printing limited to fifty signed copies. Look at the signature at the bottom. That's in Beardsley's hand; it's not part of the print."

" It looks to me like a girl being fucked by a duck," she said.

"A swan," he replied. "It's *Leda and the Swan*."

I tried to end the discussion by holding the door for Mr. Solomon, but Cora had picked up another picture. "Wow," she said. "Look at this!"

"Etching made of a Courbet painting," Solomon said. "A good one."

"But," Cora said gasping, "it's nothing but a cunt."

"Courbet called it *L'Origine du monde*," he said. "He was a French realist." Cora gave him a skeptical look. "The Origin of the World," he said, with a determined finality. With that he shut the door and locked us in.

In writing this down, I realize that exactly here, were he still alive, I would likely have given Ernest Webber a phone call. I'd have wanted to know what he could tell me about Courbet's *L'Origine du monde*. Webber never failed to have answers to my questions. Still, I rather hated to ask because I knew I'd be taking up his time and that one thing would lead to another. He'd give me a short answer, think for a while, phone me back and give me a longer answer. Then he'd do a little research and phone me a third time. For example, I'd have wanted to ask him about the model. Webber was a connoisseur of erotica, so he'd probably know. "Ernest," I'd ask, "Who posed for Courbet's *L'Origine du monde*?" He'd be smoking his pipe in his garage study where he worked, even in the winter, because his wife wouldn't allow smoking in the house. "Just a minute," he'd say. "I've got to tool my pipe." I'd wait. After a few minutes, Webber would get back on the phone. "Well, Talbot, it was Joanna Hifferman, though you'd never know it from the painting since Courbet stops just above the breasts. Remember that non-PC phrase from our teenage days, 'I could fuck her if I put a bag over her head'? That's the general idea. No head, no expression, no personality, no will. Anyway, she was Whistler's mistress, and the fact that she'd pose like that for another artist led to a terrible break between Whistler and Courbet. Can you imagine someone borrowing your girlfriend in order for her to model just her cunt? There's also a picture of her looking in a mirror—something out of that old *vanitas* tradition—called *La belle Irlandaise*. She's also the girl in Whistler's *Symphony in White*. I can't tell you a whole lot more. I've never seen the painting, just a couple of prints. There's one in The Cage up at the college. Ever seen it?" I'd have told him that it was because of that print—actually someone's etching—that I was phoning. He'd have said. "Hang on for a few minutes and I'll phone you back."

When he calls back, Webber has the giggles. "Just found out the painting was commissioned for an Ottoman diplomat introduced to Courbet when he moved to Paris from Saint Petersburg. By Saint-Beuve, no less. The guy's name is Khalil Bey, and he's already got some work by Ingres, which is fairly sexy. But Khalil Bey is ruined by his gambling habit, and he's forced to sell off his collection. At which point our Cunt is shifted from collection to collection, all over the world. It's eventually looted by Soviet troops towards the end of the Second World War, then sold to Baron Ferenc Hatvany, and taken back to Paris where it's sold for 1.5 million francs. Would you believe that it ended up in the collection of Jacques Lacan? When Lacan died, the French government allowed his family to pay his inheritance tax with Joanna Hifferman's cunt. Like a lot of famous paintings, the story of this one is quite remarkable. After that…"

But I interrupt at this point and say, "Ernest, that's really more than I need to know. I just wanted to know who the model was."

"Oh, right," says Webber. "Have you read James Walton's latest novel? I think it's his best yet. I think it's so good that I'll buy you a copy and drop it off in your mailbox. Did you ever follow my suggestion and get in touch with Jay about the archive? It would be a treasure, Talbot, a treasure." Then he puts down the phone.

Alas, this conversation never happened. Instead, I went to Wikipedia and looked up the information that I've attributed to Webber. I also Googled *L'Origine du monde*, and up popped Joanna Hifferman's cunt. It's an amazing world, this electronic window on the world. As I was on line, I also Googled "Naked Women" to see what happened. Astonishing! There were literally hundreds of links. So this is what the kids do instead of going to restricted sections in the archives like the one at OSU I visited with Cora in 1959. I wonder if Cora looks at these things on the Internet. I wonder if Cora is still alive. (Ernest Webber, of course, is no longer alive; nor are many other people I have known.) Internet sites like the one I've just visited may in time make archives and archivists like me obsolete; but not, I hope, Socialists and Jews. It was shortly after Cora and I visited the OSU archive that I made an appointment with Robert Weingarten, a rabbi I'd known for a long time, at the Upper Arlington Reform Synagogue.

The rabbi played golf with my father and Paul McNamara, a smart lawyer but, in fact, an anti-Semite. He was a smart enough lawyer to keep his bigotry to himself, but the rabbi saw through him anyway. He didn't care. The rabbi liked a good game of golf and somehow managed to enjoy McNamara's company who in turn somehow seemed to enjoy the rabbi's company. Weingarten was a very worldly man. As far as my father was concerned, it was enough that the rabbi was of the "Reform" persuasion, not super "Orthodox," and dressed like everyone else, whether on the golf course or elsewhere, without wearing a Yarmulke. And he liked the rabbi's sense of humor, which often consisted of jokes about Jews. As I've said, it was 1959. My father and McNamara played with the rabbi at the Municipal course because Upper Arlington Country Club didn't admit Jews. I would rage and storm about this at home. My father only said, "Weingarten prefers the Municipal course."

When I went to see the rabbi at the Synagogue he was well aware of my enthusiasms and intentions. After some preliminary pleasantries, he introduced the object of my visit himself. "Talbot," he said. "This wanting to become Jewish! It's the funniest thing I've ever heard."

"That's exactly what Cora said," I replied.

"She's right," said the rabbi. "Look, I know your father. I even knew your grandfather. Your mother is one of my favorite ladies in town. You're an only child. Don't rock the boat—understand? You've got a good situation. You've got connections and you're smart. And what's this I've heard about wanting to be an archivist? That's even funnier than wanting to be a Jew."

"That's also exactly what Cora said."

"What was your high school sport?"

"I didn't have a high-school sport. I liked books."

"You know," he said. "That worried your father as far back as when you were a sophomore or junior. He thought you could at least *try* to play something—hell, even soccer or volleyball. One of those sissy sports. But you were always up in your room reading books. He even thought you might be queer."

"Oh no," I said. "Let's not get started on that. Anyway, there are no Jewish queers, right?"

"Wrong, Talbot. There are plenty of Jewish queers, but that's not the point. I don't want you to become a Jewish anything. It's just not you. You're a thirty-third degree Goy, the same way your dad's a thirty-third degree Mason. Right at the top. That's not something you want to give up because you think Jews are smart. You're a smart Goy, so be a smart Goy. But don't come around here telling me you want to be Jewish or I'll send you off to some awful Kibbutz in Israel where they'll work your ass so hard you'll be sorry you aren't a Nazi. Also, you've got a beautiful girlfriend who somehow sticks it out with you in spite of your crazy obsession. I'll bet she's even fucking you, right? You're a lucky kid. Don't be a stupid Yid. We've got enough of those. I have to deal with them day-in, day-out. I'm a serious man, Talbot, in spite of my jocular manner—a professional, and proud of it. If I'm still alive in ten years time and you come back in here still telling me you want to be Jewish, I'll help you out. But I don't think that's going to happen. About the archivist thing, there's nothing I can do. That part's not my responsibility. Oh, and Philip Roth's not your man. You should be reading Updike instead. And Henry Miller's not as good as you think. And Talbot, one last thing—go out to the Arlington Club and learn to play golf. Now get out of my office and give my love to your mom and dad."

I went on reading Philip Roth and Henry Miller. Roth's *Goodbye, Columbus*, after all, addressed my situation so directly I almost had the sense that the author had dropped through my chimney like Santa Claus to take up residence in my house. Published in 1959, my first year with Cora and my first year at OSU, it mocked the brother of Brenda Patimkin who had attended Ohio State and who in the title story of Roth's now-famous debut collection repeatedly plays a nostalgic phonograph record from OSU ending "Goodbye, Columbus, Goodbye, Ohio State!" The brother is an assimilated rube. Brenda is Neil Klugman's upper-class girlfriend, and Neil is a working-class Jew from Newark. Much of the plot turns on whether or not Brenda is going to have a diaphragm fitted, a question I kept raising with Cora at the very time I discovered the book. The more my studies faltered because of the sheer exhaustion of having sex with Cora every night, the more I began to fear that she *wanted* to get pregnant. (Neither of us liked condoms, and sometimes I wouldn't wear one.) Part of my exhaustion had to do with the lack of a proper venue for our lovemaking. We both lived at home. This left us with the back seat of my Studebaker Lark and the occasional apartment of an acquaintance. As Cora became more and more demanding of my time,

I began to get scared—but it took literally four years to get as scared as I should have been from the start. By that time people assumed we were getting married, and soon.

Laymen didn't know in those days how to recognize bipolar disorders, or how to help people who had them. I just thought Cora was moody. But in fact she'd get so high—no drugs, no alcohol—that she'd do things like run screaming through the library shouting my name and variations on it like "Talbot Eastmate! Whoever knew anyone called Talbot. Talbot Bookmark, Talbot Mountbank, Talbot Yuckmoist. What a ridiculous name! Where's my Talbot, baby?" She spent some time at a private mental clinic. She tried to kill herself twice, once with some of her mother's tranquilizers and once, when we went to a Lake Michigan beach together, by swimming as far out into the lake as she could in order to drown herself from exhaustion. I am myself a bad swimmer, but I managed to get out to her with a child's air mattress in hand which I finally persuaded her to catch hold of as we had a discussion of metaphysics and existentialism while treading water for half an hour before finally kicking into shore clutching the toy. The angry kid from whom I had taken it stood knee-deep in the lake, glaring at us as we huffed and puffed and tried to catch our breath.

When I phoned Ernest Webber asking for help on some of my stories about Timothy Westmont, he tried, at first, to be polite. I had no one else to show them to, so Webber was stuck being my only reader.

"That's a funny moment," he said, "when your character Westmont gets his hand stuck in the teapot. But you ought to be careful making sport with the woman who has a withered arm. You've got to be as good as Flannery O'Connor for that sort of thing. If you published this, everybody at the college would recognize Georgia Steiner. That wouldn't be cool. You'd even be taking a chance on a lawsuit. And then there's the tone. It's kind of adolescent, don't you think? For a man of seventy, I'd say it lacks a certain dignity. Sorry, Talbot, but you asked. And what's our friend Diana Adams going to think about the wife? What's the point of embarrassing her?"

"Ernest," I said, "it's fiction."

There was a pause while Webber relit his pipe at the other end of the phone and took a couple of puffs. He was never in a hurry. Pipe smoking is a lost art among intellectuals. It made for such a wonderful rhythm in a long conversation. Back in 1959, even I smoked a pipe after I noticed that Joel Barkan's father did. Harvey Goldberg smoked a pipe.

And Rabbi Weingarten. But in the end, smoking killed two of them. Now and then I'll catch the scent of someone's pipe at a bar or coffee-house where smoking is still permitted. It smells somehow both of sex and death. I breathe it in with pleasure and a sense of the forbidden.

"Fiction," Webber said. "Of course, my friend. Look, your thing is old and dusty papers. The older the better. Put this Westmont stuff in the archive and let somebody find it in fifty years. Then it might be really interesting, at least as history."

Webber could be tough. He was an even sterner critic of my reading than he was of my writing. He read Defoe, Dickens, the Brontës, George Eliot, Henry James, Thomas Mann (in German), Flaubert (in French), Joyce, Nabokov, and James Walton. His characteristic self-deprecation led him to joke that he was totally out of it, never even knew where to begin with contemporaries (and his use of "contemporary" was comically intended to refer to my own anachronistic sense of it). He'd say things like, "Is Salinger any good, do you think? What about Norman Mailer?" But I knew he thought that nothing I read with enthusiasm would last. And he was amused (but also really sorry) that I maintained my youthful excitement about the writers I'd grown up with. Because we were good friends, I could say things like, "I'd love to actually meet Philip Roth some day." He'd chew his pipe, wait a minute or two, and reply: "Talbot, you wouldn't." He'd pause on the phone, reach for his favorite Walton, and cite: "*Margaret's Book*, page 72." After our conversation I'd of course check the reference. Have a look in your own copy where Byron, the hero, says to Margaret about "people like us" and "those we fancy to be great." I'll probably have to quote it later on. Now and then I'd remind Webber that James Walton was not only a "contemporary," but that he lived in our own small college town. "Walton," he'd say, "is an exception to every rule." Then he'd hang up, leaving me to figure out what he meant.

In the absence of friends at Ohio State, I continued to talk now and then to Rabbi Weingarten about my problems with Cora. He was willing to listen, just so I agreed to avoid the subject of wanting to be Jewish. He was torn, eventually, by his admiration of Cora's astonishing beauty and his growing acknowledgment that she was clearly crazy, suicidal, and therefore probably not the girl for me to marry. He deeply regretted having come round to this conclusion. He'd say, "Talbot, I'm not a shrink. I'm also an old guy like your father and all his lawyer pals. You need a friend your own age. Now that Cora's been in college herself for a couple of years, isn't there someone who knows you both and can give you the kind of help you need?" I told him there wasn't, really. He was amazed that someone could go through an entire undergraduate career without a single close friend. Three years had passed since our famous conversation about becoming a Jew shortly after the relationship with Cora had begun. He'd said that if I still wanted his help about the temporarily forbidden subject in ten years' time, I could then reintroduce it. I had a sense on these visits that he was nervously consulting his calendar. It was now already 1962.

I was also increasingly having to deal with Cora's parents. I couldn't tell whether they hoped I'd soon take a difficult problem off their hands, or just hoped I'd go away to graduate school and not be forever hanging around their house. I was there more than I was at home, and of course any conversation with them was increasingly difficult since I mainly wanted them out of the house so Cora and I could have sex in their bed, which was bigger and better than hers. When the crisis finally came that precipitated my break with Cora, it was initiated by her mother. I received a phone call one late afternoon from her mom asking me to come over. The houses were only a few blocks away, so over I trotted, thinking this was going to be about some arrangement for a dinner or event on the town as we sometimes did things all together as a kind of family. But I was wrong. Cora's mother met me at the door with a stern expression, and reached out with something, saying "Is this yours?" It looked like the foil from a stick of chewing gum until I suddenly saw it was a condom wrapper.

"I imagine it is," I said.

"Talbot," she said. "I found this in OUR bed! I've taken you for a serious and responsible man. So has my husband. What are we supposed to make of this?"

"It's a sign that I'm a serious and responsible man," I said.

"Talbot!" she exclaimed.

When I told the rabbi this story, he burst out laughing. "That's telling the old Goy," he laughed. "Will this be the end of the affair?" I'd never thought of it as an "affair"; Cora was just my girlfriend. What did in fact end it, whatever it was, occurred only a few weeks later. I'd by that time received notification that I had been admitted to the library science program at Stanford. Shortly after I'd told Cora, she was walking through campus with a copy of Henry Miller's *Tropic of Capricorn* under her arm. Some passing man noticed this, chatted her up, took her for coffee, discussed Henry Miller for an hour, and then took her back to his apartment and fucked her. The Rabbi thought this was really funny, too. "And all this is entirely your own fault, Talbot," he said. "Who would have thought your introduction to the joys of library science would have led her to this. It's what they call 'poetic justice,' my friend. I'm really sorry for you, but perhaps it's all for the best. Get yourself out to Stanford and have a good life."

When I started to leave, he got out of his chair and gave me a big crushing bear hug. I think he had tears in his eyes.

*

By some strange coincidence or synchronicity, I've just returned from Columbus, Ohio. I received a phone call from the Director of Education at the Ohio State House telling me that the Supreme Court Chambers would be moved into a new building soon and that the portraits of my father and grandfather would go into storage, perhaps never to emerge into the light of day again. Did I want to see them before this happened? I said I did. Some time before receiving the call, I had also received a letter—the old-fashioned kind, in an envelope with a stamp—from Peter Robinson, a childhood friend whose name I borrowed for the story "Westmont and Tar Hollow Camp," telling me that Glen Echo Park, the Columbus ravine where he and I had played as kids and which figures importantly in my stories about Timothy Westmont, was going to be rededicated by the Franklin County Park Department. He was going to go. Did I want to meet him "down the glen?" I pulled out the letter to check the date, which was May 14th, Bastille Day. I took that as a good omen, emailed Pete, emailed the lady at the State House, and went.

It has been fifty years since I've seen the portraits of my two judicial forebears. My grandfather served on the Ohio Supreme Court longer than anyone ever had before him, and his record still stands. When he died at the age of 83, falling from the third-story window where he was trying to show exterminators where squirrels got into his house, he was still on the bench and still writing ground-breaking opinions. In the newspapers of his era, he was always called "The Dean of Ohio Judges." To me he was remote and intimidating, but he indulged me about one thing—books. He had an enormous private library with *Ex Libris* plates in every volume, many dating from the days when he lived in Van Wert, Ohio in the first decades of the 20th century and people with libraries loaned out their books to each other. He always made it clear to me that

I could borrow as many books as I liked, just so I made sure to tell him what I thought after I had read them. My "book reports" constituted rare moments with the Great Man. On these occasions, and these occasions only, he would listen with great patience as I told him what I thought of Robert Louis Stevenson or Sir Walter Scott or James Fennimore Cooper. When I was finished, he'd pat me on the head, smile, and say "Keep reading, Talbot; keep reading, my boy. " And I did.

My father was a poor shadow of "The Dean of Ohio Judges." When his father died, he ran for the unexpired term and won the election against three other candidates. Most people who voted for him thought they were voting for his father. He understood this, of course, and he managed to win three further terms in office for the same reason. He was unhappy on the Supreme Court, and should have stayed at the Municipal level hearing traffic cases. His portrait is bland and photographic. My grandfather's, at least, looks like a painting. It's typical, given his ego, that he rejected the first two paintings that were done. I have no idea who paid for three separate artists to attempt the "likeness" as he referred to it, but the other paintings still exist and are now in my cousin's basement. They seem to me just as good as the one that's hanging in the chambers and about to go into storage. "Vanity, saith the preacher," and all that. But given my line of work I'm sure I'll end up with one or another of the portraits, doubtless paid for by the college archive's budget. In fact I'll probably figure a way to get all three of them.

When I got back home, I wanted to tell Ernest Webber about my trip, especially the unexpected evening I'd spent at Johnny's 402 Club. Johnny's was the jazz club where Joel Barkan and I spent much of our senior year in high school. I'd often told Webber about our times there in 1959, and he, an encyclopedic authority on jazz of every kind, was sometimes even a little impressed. In spite of my bookish disposition, I listened to lots of jazz in the late '50s and early '60s, just before the Beatles and Dylan arrived on the scene and the jazz clubs all folded. Within weeks of each other, I heard the Miles Davis Quintet when John Coltrane was with it, the Jazz Messengers, the Modern Jazz Quartet, Charles Mingus, Dave Brubeck, Ahmad Jamal, and many others of that generation. Joel and I were under age, so we carried false IDs, wore bop shades, and smoked pipes in order to look anonymous. We were also usually the only two white faces in an all black club. More than that, my father had sent Johnny, the owner, into prison more than once for numbers racketeering. I'd tell my parents that I was going to the library, a very plausible lie given my official enthusiasms. Then I'd hit the 402 with Joel.

I was just telling Webber the whole story on the phone. I reminded him about my high school nights on the town and told him that after Pete Robinson and I met at the Glen Echo Park rededication I checked the phone book to see if the 402 still existed. After a very hot afternoon in the ravine, I persuaded Pete to join me for a night at the club. Pete's not a great jazz fan, but he's usually up for a good time, so he agreed to come along after a quick dinner we had together near The Glen. As I've just told Webber, I was amazed that Johnny's still existed and that I happened to be in town the very week when Jimmy Heath was playing there. As Webber well knew, Jimmy Heath is one of the survivors of the bebop generation. He goes as far back as Charlie Parker and Dizzy Gillespie. He's 85, and tough as my grandfather was before he fell out that window. His younger brother, Albert Tootie, still plays the drums with his quartet, but Percy, who played with his group after he left the Modern Jazz Quartet, has recently died. This was news to Webber.

"Who's playing bass?" he asked.

"David Wong," I said. "Straight from Julliard."

"It figures," he said. "They're all conservatory trained these days. What about the piano?"

"Jeb Patton," I said. "Studied with Sir Roland Hanna at Queens."

"You know," said Webber, "I probably saw The Jazz Messengers twenty or thirty times, always with new sidemen. That used to be the jazz university. I'm not keen on these academic kids, even Wynton, whose Lincoln Center thing is a kind of jazz museum. The real evolution of jazz has basically ended. Like that of the novel."

I didn't want to get into Webber's theories about the end of jazz, the end of the novel, the end of art. He was always pessimistic. So I told him a little about Glen Echo Park. He had met Pete once or twice, and was amused by the fact that as a very young dentist at a D.C. military hospital he had worked on both Eisenhower and General Omar Bradley. He mentioned this.

"Yes," I said. "And on General Westmorland as well."

"I hope he pulled out all of Westmorland's teeth," he said. You won't remember Westmorland, but he was the commanding general in Vietnam. Webber and I had been anti-war in those days.

"Speaking of chops," he said. "What about Jimmy Heath?"

"Dentures," I laughed. "They literally slipped out during a solo. Cool as can be, he nodded to Patton, who took a solo as he slipped them back in place. Then he said to the audience, "False teeth, man. If you're not there yet I'm happy for you." Pete Robinson started laughing so hard that we had to leave the club. It's still all black, by the way, except that night for me and Pete and two of the guys in the band."

"What did they play?" asked Webber. I reeled them off: "*Changes, Wall to Wall, You or Me, Autumn in New York, The Rio Dawn,* and *From a Lonely Bass*—an elegy for Percy."

"I always liked Percy Heath," he said.

"So did I."

As you know, I couldn't really have had this conversation with my old friend because he's dead. And yet somehow I just did. I also went on at length about my nostalgia for the old ravine. I told him how it amazed me in retrospect how free we all were to roam where we would from dawn until dusk. Pete Robinson's memories are even better than my own. Pete and I shook our heads over how unlikely it would be to have this freedom today. Down the ravine we'd go, and who knew what we were going to do or when we'd come back. Kids today always seem to have closely managed and monitored activities. We had nothing but freedom—which was everything—freedom of a kind I haven't experienced since. No one thought we'd be abducted or murdered. If we got hurt, and we often did, we'd get patched up or sent back out to play. If there were tough kids down the ravine, we'd steer clear of them. In the winter we'd come back sopping wet and freezing cold from sledding in what often became watery slush. We'd take a bath—not a shower—and warm up with a cup of hot chocolate. Even during "polio season" no one seemed to worry (though I knew people who had caught and survived this awful illness). When we went to the Hudson movie theater on a Saturday morning, we'd stay all day, eating nothing but popcorn and candy bars. Having seen the double feature once, we'd get some more popcorn, another candy bar, and see the double feature again. And I told Webber about the old house—a simple frame dwelling (now covered in siding) with a kitchen, dining room and living room on the first floor and three bedrooms on the second. The door that we used was on the Arcadia side, except in the spring when birds would inevitably nest in the lilac bushes that spilled over one part of the small porch. Then we used the door on the Glen Echo side until the fledglings had flown. I can even remember the old rotary telephone number (Jefferson 3332). In the back, opening out from the living room, was a large screened porch that stretched the entire width of the house. We spent as much time on the porch as possible, especially in the hot summers before air conditioning. Sometimes we even slept on the porch, trying to keep cool. The back yard was fairly large and ended just behind two wonderful oak trees that grew to a great height only a few feet from each other.

Delivery men of all kinds came to the Arcadia door: milk man, bread man, grocery boy from the small grocery store on Summit, paper boy, strawberry man with a wonderful street cry that took one back to the Middle Ages, even an ice man—we had an ice box at first, and not a proper refrigerator—and various odd job men looking for work. My father in those days was a Municipal Court judge, and he would sometimes hire people he had sentenced to jail to work in the yard once they'd been released. I found these "criminals" all very exciting and spent a lot of time talking to them. They were predictably enough embarrassed when I'd ask them enthusiastically to describe their crimes with my father standing near by. I got to know some of them pretty well. I hated it when we moved to Arlington in 1958.

I asked Webber if he'd read my Westmont story about Glen Echo, the one in which my character is deprived of his paradise and sent off to a summer camp.

"I don't think you've shown me that one, Talbot," he said.

"Well, I said, young Timothy spends idyllic summers during the late 1940s and early '50s playing with his visiting cousins from Washington, D.C. in the Glen Echo Park. They improvise stories of knights or pirates and deck themselves in costumes and paraphernalia from Westmont's hoard of hats, capes, plumes, boots, jackets, and a collection of family heirlooms, including his grandfather's Spanish American War swords and his uncle's uniforms from the First World War. I've got a photograph somewhere in the archive where you see Timothy on the left with his three-cornered hat, cape, sword, and wide belt, along with his cousin Robert, similarly attired. I think this was all for the Captain Horatio Hornblower game. Are you there, Webber?"

"It turns out to be a sad summer for Westmont when the cousins sign up for an organized camp near their home and cease their annual summer visits to Columbus. Hold on, I think I've got the page right here. Are you there? *He could see for himself what was coming. Although he held out for a year, he finally agreed that he would follow Robert and Richard into what was represented to him as a way to meet new friends and learn new skills at an organized camp of his own. But he knew it was mainly an unwanted initiation into proper adolescence. He had loved being a child.*

"Ernest, are you there? Webber?"

*

When I got to Stanford in 1963, the first person I met was Koba Steinberg. You'll think Koba is an African name, but it's Russian; in fact it was the most used of Joseph Stalin's *noms de guerre* in the early days of the revolution. Koba's parents were unregenerate Stalinists from the 1930s. Koba wasn't himself a Stalinist, or even an active socialist. He was a romantic, self-mythologizing biker out of the early poems of Thom Gunn. He was also a brilliant student, having been an undergraduate at Princeton. Like Cora, he found it hilarious that I had come to Stanford to study library science and wanted to be an archivist. He took me to my first ever rock'n'roll show at the San Francisco Cow Palace. He almost got me to try LSD. That first day we met, he let me know at once, amazing me, that he had taken creative writing courses with Philip Roth. And he loved it that I was from Columbus, Ohio. "Oh me oh my oh, Why did I ever leave Ohio," he'd intone. And then he'd say, quoting Ron Patimkin's OSU graduation yearbook LP: "Goodbye, Columbus... Goodbye, Ohio State..." I was able to toss back at him a quote from the eventually revolted Neil Klugman when he finally realizes that he can't possibly marry Ron's sister Brenda, in part because of her ghastly family: "Ron Patimkin! Thee, brother-in-law!" The funny thing is that Koba Steinberg almost became my own—brother-in-law, that is.

Koba was not an ordinary graduate student, but a member of the Wallace Stegner Writing Program, an opportunity for already published writers to live in the Stanford community, audit some courses if they liked, meet together once a week, and work for two years on their current project without having people bother them about exams, degrees, or anything else. I envied him enormously as I signed up for "Bibliography 401." Koba had published a few short stories in respectable journals, but didn't seem to be especially pleased about that. What pleased him was that the Stegner program stipend paid him enough to afford the Harley he'd just bought, and that while at Princeton he had written some songs that were now being performed by some of the leading rock groups. The names of the groups meant nothing to me at all: he'd mention "The Dead," "The Spoonful," "The Airplane," "Hendrix," and so on. None of it made any sense to me. I only knew about Elvis. When he took me to the Cow Palace, I spent most of my time being frightened of the enormous crowd. It was like a British football crowd about to get out of control and trample people under their feet. The music, if indeed it was music at all, was very loud. A lot of the groups were really old men, the first generation of rockers. Now I only remember someone called "Little Richard." Or was it "Little Robert." Anyway, I hated it. Koba didn't care.

"Talbot," he'd say, "we're going to rock you through your whole degree."

Trying to live on my meager scholarship in far-off Mountain View, I needed some kind of transportation. The distance between the apartment I found and the Stanford campus was too far for a bicycle. Koba inspired me to buy a Rabbit. A Rabbit was an inexpensive motor scooter like a budget version of the Italian Vespa. If a Vespa could buzz and sting, the Rabbit merely loped. But I could afford it. Taking off with Koba on our various trips was pretty funny: Koba on his Harley, me on my Rabbit. Big brother and little brother; that's how it was. Since Koba didn't really have to attend class, he'd persuade me to come along on his adventures—out to see Ken Kesey, for example, someone he inexplicably seemed to know, in the Los Altos Hills. This frightened me more than the rock concert crowd at the Cow Palace, since all of Kesey's friends seemed to be Hell's Angels at that stage, slowly being converted by the suddenly famous former Stegner Fellow (*One Flew Over the Cuckoo's Nest* was just about to be followed by *Sometimes a Great Notion*) to the Anti-War Movement. During a protest march to the Redwood City napalm plant, the Hell's Angels had attacked us all, nearly killing the best eighteenth-century bibliographer on the west coast. After Kesey had his meeting with Koba and the Angel leaders, we had, instead of their opposition, the best group of bodyguards one could possibly imagine. Koba sometimes rode with the Angels himself. I couldn't figure out, in fact, why he bothered spending time with me. "I like you, Talbot," he'd say. "I get that, Koba," I'd reply. "Who," he'd say, "can explain friendship or love?"

Love came along a second time in my life in 1963. Koba's sister arrived in San Francisco to live in the Haight-Ashbury, and we were introduced. More than that, we were introduced in a gas-lit apartment where a Stegner Fellow lived who had parties every other weekend. This one was shortly after Thanksgiving, and everybody was keen on a new LP by a rock group called "The Beatles." This time, as I admitted to Koba, I liked the sound. It wasn't jazz, and it wasn't Mozart, but I could understand—I could hear—that it was different from run-of-the-mill popular music, which I loathed. Somehow Koba's sister emerged directly out of the big hit from the band's first LP, "I Saw Her Standing There." I heard it and immediately saw her, shimmering and available. Koba didn't even have to introduce us. Someone else did. "Hey, Talbot," someone said, "Meet Koba's sister. She's an amazing bird." Bird. I didn't know the person who introduced us, but he must have been a Brit. (The only "bird" I was ever introduced to again was Diana Adams, a woman I met some years later in England and a travesty of whom I kind of married to

148

Timothy Westmont in one of my stories.) Koba's sister was Jenny, and when the stranger introduced us, she kissed me as if I were her long-term lover, tongue in my mouth, her hand on my crotch. As I write this, and I've mentioned it before, I'm 70 years old. It turns me on, I can tell you, dredging up these memories. Where is Jenny? Should I "Google" her? (But how many times has she changed her name? After what eventually happened, I'd better not even try.) Once I realized that Jenny had other suitors, I'd beg Koba for help. "Your biker friends," I told him, "are all chasing your sister. What the hell am I supposed to do?"

I attended my classes, worrying. You'll understand that there wasn't a single computer involved in library science in those days at the very place where in a few decades Apple would be founded by a couple of Stanford types and then Google a little later. Where my student slum digs were located in Mountain View you now find the very control center of Silicon Valley, with all of its eyes and ears. In 1963 I did have one technological distraction to consider—the Stanford linear accelerator that was pointed directly at my apartment and stopped only a mile or so away. You could see it plainly on your way to the beach, under a very long earthwork that looked like Ohio's Serpent Mound straightened out and extended. I'd sit studying the history of the Dewey Decimal System wondering what kind of particle they were firing at me on that particular day all the way from where the accelerator began on the coast. I'd sit there listening to the Mahler Ninth Symphony on the old Bruno Walter recording, a gift, amazingly enough, from Koba. He didn't just like rock'n'roll, it turned out, but he was very secretive about some of his personal tastes. As a jazz fan, I was new to Mahler, Shostakovich, Bartók, and other modern composers Koba shared with me. Jenny was strictly a rocker, and so when she started coming to my apartment I put away not only my jazz records, but also her own brother's classics.

Jenny was never exactly a student. She'd take the odd course at San Francisco State or one of the local junior colleges, then drop it halfway through the semester, and go back to smoking pot or snorting cocaine in the room where she lived in the Haight-Ashbery. Soon enough, she started "renting" a room at Koba's place. As far as I can remember she never had a job. Like Koba himself, she was a creature of the Sixties, and for long periods of time she just hung out here and there, often in my bed. She'd arrive in the afternoon and use the key I eventually had made for her. When I returned from my courses, there she'd be, listening to her own LPs on my stereo, smoking her dope. I'd make something for dinner on the old gas stove and, as often as not, Koba would come by just as we were about to eat. He had a great appetite—for food, as for everything else—so Jenny and I would end up pushing half our own servings full of fried rice and frozen peas onto his plate. Koba would bring the wine, or sometimes a six-pack of beer. We'd drink, eat, and listen to his stories. Unlike me, he was very much a social being and immediately made lots of friends. Among them were the young writers, mostly poets in the regular Ph.D. program, soon to make a considerable stir on the literary scene—Robert Hass, Robert Pinsky, James McMichael, John Peck, and John Matthias. As a prose writer, he seemed to envy poets, and he made it a point to audit the courses then being taught by the irascible Yvor Winters. Winters may have been forgotten by now—I really have no way of knowing—but in those days he was still regarded by the poetry establishment as a ferocious threat to most of what they stood for. He was also dying—from cancer of the tongue—which made all of his late pronouncements sound like something spoken by an oracle. Koba especially liked Hass' early poems, which he said showed every sign of becoming major work. He was indifferent to the work of Pinsky, McMichael and Peck, although he liked the poets themselves well enough, but positively disliked Matthias, whose grad-student poems he thought were merely academic. He'd go on about this group and maybe a recent trip to Big Sur. He claimed to know Henry Miller and, through him, Anaïs Nin. In fact he claimed he'd "fucked Miss Nin with pleasure, even though she's an old lady." At this, Jenny would say: "Koba, please keep these things in the family." I laughed at this, thinking she meant the stories.

Koba claimed to have written Everly Brothers songs when he was only sixteen. I barely remembered the Everly Brothers, and so my response wasn't what he'd expected. (I've just Googled these brothers: "Bye Bye Love," "Wake Up Little Suzie": those were the songs he was proud to have written.) But when he said he knew Christopher Isherwood and a lot of his friends in L.A., I perked up. The Stanford archive, in fact, included some Isherwood papers, and I had great respect for those parts of the journals I'd seen, though I had less interest in the novels. The journals were a kind of three-dimensional x-ray of four decades of intellectual life in the U.K. and U.S., an archivist's dream. The main thing, as I saw it, was that Isherwood should be persuaded not to publish them. If he did, those thousands of pages would lose all value to someone like me. You have to understand that Isherwood's "friends" were not all gay, as I think has been generally assumed. Even at the playwright Jerome Lawrence's

Malibu house a few months later I met an amazingly seductive group of young girls, all of whom said they were "actresses," and that they had come along with "Chris." Koba—I was tagging along, as usual—kept telling me that not a single one of them was a match for "our Jenny."

Koba commented very early on in our relationship that he could understand me best as someone who really preferred books to people. (I've attributed this characteristic, of course, to Westmont in my stories. It's the real key to his troubles.) Koba didn't say this with any kind of annoyance at all, but just as if he were commenting on the weather. It's the way things were. He was sorry, but he liked me anyway. He asked me once if I'd ever like to have students and I told him frankly that I wouldn't. What I liked was working with the papers and, when you got right down to it, I wasn't all that keen to share them with anyone else. Koba wasn't much interested in my enthusiasm for the Isherwood journals, Isherwood being in his view just a Hollywood hireling. What really hooked him into my own activities was the news that I'd been asked to do some donkey-work for Alexander Kerensky in the Hoover Institute. Yes, *that* Alexander Kerensky.

Since nobody studies history any longer, I suppose I need to explain that Alexander Feodorovich Kerensky was briefly, at the young age of 36, head of the Russian provisional government after the March revolution of 1917. To everyone's amazement, the last Romanov Tsar, Alexander II, suddenly abdicated as a result of his own incompetence and a few massive street demonstrations. But Kerensky's moment on the world stage was very brief indeed. Lenin, for whom Kerensky's own father had once written a letter of recommendation—he was principal of the provincial high school attended both by his son and the future communist leader—arrived in the famous sealed train and chased Stanford's 1963 scholar-in-residence out of the Petersburg Winter Palace dressed as a nun or a Muslim woman wearing a burqa—or something like that; the stories vary. Anyway, without anyone paying much attention, he had lived out an exile's life in France and the U.S., to end up in the Hoover Institute archive shuffling his papers and sending me on endless errands to look up this and that, usually manuscripts and books written in a language I couldn't read. Koba thought Kerensky had been dead for many years. At last I was able to tell some stories that he and Jenny listened to. Their father, the Stalinist, was still living in a New York federal lockup. They knew their Russian history.

So does Ernest Webber, who knows just about everything. I told him once about a phone call I received at around that time—or, rather, two phone calls in a row, and he enjoyed the story. It went a little like this: Jenny is spending the night in my flat when, out of the blue, Cora phones from Columbus. I've not heard from her for months, but, since Jenny answers the phone, I don't realize for a while that Cora is on the line. It's late; we're both jerked into full consciousness by the ringing. The conversation, from my side of the bed sounds something like this (blanks, of course, indicating what I can't hear): "Hello?" _____. "Jenny." _____. "I suppose you could say that." _____. "Why is that any of your business?" _____. "Okay, Okay, sure I'm the new girlfriend." _____. "You want to talk to him, he's right here." _____. "No, we're not." _____. "Yes we have been, but we're all done with that now. I'm smoking some dope and he's reading a book." _____. _____. _____. To me: "She wants to know what book you're reading." Me, to Jenny: "Sir Hilary Jenkinson's *Manual of the Archive of the Deputy Keeper of the British Public Records Office, 1922.*" Jenny, to me: "You're kidding." Me, To Jenny: "It's really very good." "He's reading Sir Hilary Jenkinson's *Manual of the Archive of the Deputy Keeper of the British Public Records Office, 1922.* _____. "That's what he says." _____. _____. _____. "Yeah, I'll tell him." To me: "She says she really misses you." Me, to Jenny: "Say I miss her too. At least now and then." _____. _____. To me: "She says that last bit really pisses her off." Me, to Jenny: "Say I'm deeply sorry to hear that." Jenny: "I think she just hung up."

You must imagine my gestures occupying the blank spaces above during my re-enactment of the conversation for Webber's amusement. Shrugged shoulders, hands in the air, little fists. Then I tell him about the next phone call. By then Jenny and I have both just fallen asleep. Jenny, for whom sleeping was always a difficulty, answers the phone with some irritation. "If this is Cora," she said, "just fuck off. We're both asleep." _____. _____. _____. "He says it's your boss." Me, to Jenny: "My boss?" Jenny into the phone: "He doesn't seem to get it. Who's speaking?" _____! Jenny, to me: "Alexander Feodorovich Kerensky."

Webber thinks this is all pretty funny because he knows about Kerensky's career at Stanford. At the time, Jenny was just appalled. For her, this was a family matter. Her parents were Marxist-Leninists, and her father would gladly have assassinated Kerensky had he been in Petersburg in 1917. She and Koba had grown up on stories about my boss' escape dressed in his burqa or nun's veil. She couldn't believe I was working for the guy. But I was learning a lot, and besides it paid me some extra pocket money to top up my stipend. Webber is also keen to hear my stories about Jenny and Koba, but I tell him I'll save those for some boring wedding or funeral down the line. Ernest, I'm afraid you wouldn't have liked either of them. I see you chewing on your pipe, then rubbing your temples. You say something like, "Sounds to me as if they were a couple of phonies." But we never did get round to this conversation, did we, though we seem to have attended plenty of weddings and, more and more, far too many funerals. That's why I have to tell you about them here.

In the end I preferred Kerensky to Jenny, just as in the end I preferred Rabbi Weingarten and Harvey Goldberg to Cora. You'll understand this. It turned out that the former president of the provisional government lived in the same modest rooming house as John Matthias and a fiction writer in the Stegner program with Koba, Richard Elman. Not Richard Ellmann, the Joyce biographer. This Richard Elman was a fairly successful novelist and for a while did a regular show on National Public Radio. He was a great raconteur, and described to us (Jenny, Koba, Matthias, and myself) the way Kerensky behaved at his—Elman's—wedding reception in the boarding-house garden:

"You know, the A.K. who shared a bathroom with Matthias and me in the home of Herbert Hoover's niece was known as a sore looser. You'd be one, too, if you were chased out of the Winter Palace like he was. But worse than that, he was a dreadful snob. Also, of course, a charmer, a hand kisser, a well-oiled mechanical doll with a set of fine steel Swiss watch springs in his elbows and knees. He would do his morning constitutional heel and toe fashion, as if taking part in the Coney Island marathon. Not once but twice I caught him peering down a sun-freckled bosom as he bent from hand to hand in my landlady's back garden at the reception. Having known the splendors of Petersburg society, Nicolai's court, the great world of the moneyed exiles, it was absolutely splendid of A.K. to be trying so hard not to condescend to my wedding reception. He flitted from barbecue pit to beer case as if at an Imperial *levée*." Eventually, Elman wrote up his A.K. anecdotes in a book called *Namedropping*. I've seen a copy in the college library.

Though from my point of view Elman doesn't describe Kerensky at all, that's not really the point. The point is that all the time Jenny was mocking my archival ambitions, Kerensky was supportive and enthusiastic. He had himself long since disappeared from the world of international politics to the stacks, carels and special collections of the

British Museum (sitting, perhaps, just where Marx himself had read and studied), the Paris Bibliothèque Nationale, the New York Public Library, and now the Hoover Institute. He had become, in Melville's terms, a library cormorant, and he recognized and rewarded the like-minded. Before long I was being invited to his apartment in the rooming house for Russian vodka and glasses of good French wine. We'd talk about the Vietnam war and the Civil Rights Movement. To a certain extent he lived in the past, but he also kept up on the current world scene. And he expected you to know who he was. Poor Matthias, for example, confused his name with that of a Russian symphony conductor, and was on the outs with Kerensky from that moment on. Elman was smarter, but was also a smart-ass and aggressive Sixties lefty. He wanted to goad the old man into anti-Soviet tirades, which was easy to do. I tried to listen rather than talk, and to do the basic tasks he asked me to perform as efficiently as possible. The more time we spent together the more Jenny and Koba taunted me. Jenny especially liked to recite some lines from "The Hunting of the Snark":

> They returned hand-in-hand, and the Bellman, unmanned
>   (For a moment) with noble emotion,
> Said "This amply repays all the wearisome days
>   We have spent on the billowy ocean!"

> Such friends, as the Beaver and Butcher became,
>   Have seldom if ever been known;
> In winter or summer, 'twas always the same—
>   You could never meet either alone.

"You're calling Kerensky a butcher?" I asked. "Pretty strange given the monster your family supported in the 1930s."

"No, I'm just calling you a beaver," Jenny said. "You can make up any kind of butcher you like. You're aware of his scholarly habits." And she recited another stanza of "The Snark":

> The Beaver brought paper, portfolio, pens,
>   And ink in unfailing supplies:
> While strange creepy creatures came out of their dens,
>   And watched them with wondering eyes.

And Koba reminded me again about the strangest creepy creature in Roth's *Goodbye, Columbus*—the one I most wanted to forget—John McKee, a student of library science at Newark State Teachers College who worked part time at a branch library with priapic Benjamin, and who "was only twenty-one, but wore elastic bands around his sleeves [and would] march starchily down the stairs to work assiduously at stamping books in and out." No one remembers this specter from the story, but he was known to our hero as "John McRubberbands." The most famous one-liner in *Goodbye, Columbus* occurs when someone asks Brenda what she's been doing during the summer and she says, "Growing a penis." If John McRubberbands had been asked the same question, he'd have certainly said that he had been sucking his own penis into his crotch in order to grow a vagina. But never mind all that.

Kerensky and Koba met only once, and I had tried very hard to prevent that meeting from happening. It was all Matthias' fault. Not understanding the extent to which the confusion between the hero of the March revolution and an émigré symphony conductor had annoyed my boss, he arranged a party at the boarding house to which, along with many other inappropriate guests, Koba, Jenny, and I had been invited. After everybody had consumed a good amount of vodka, wine, and (in Jenny's case) the best Acapulco Gold (is that right? Wasn't that the marijuana of choice?), Matthias, idiot that he was, brought Koba and Karensky together.

"Professor Kerensky," he said. (Kerensky was not a professor.) "This is my friend Koba Steinberg."

"Koba? Koba?" said Kerensky, blenching. "Surely nobody here is called Koba."

"Absolutely," Koba said. "I was named for Comrade Stalin."

"For God's sake," said Kerensky. "Why would anybody name you for him?"

"To help destroy," said Koba, "the capitalist system and bring Marx-ism-Leninism to the whole fucking U.S.A.!"

"Get this madman out of here," said Kerensky—looking around for someone who might have the authority to do that. His eyes eventually fell on me. Talbot," he said, "please remove this idiot from my apartment building."

I realized that Koba was now pretty drunk. "Come on," I said. "Let's you and me and Jenny go out for a pizza." Once out in the street by our bikes, I asked Koba why he should bother making the old man angry and confused. "It's bad enough," I said, "that he's got to live with Elman and Matthias."

Jenny said, "Let's go to Talbot's place. We'll smoke some dope and read the new poems Koba's got by Robert Hass and Pensky."

"That's Pinsky," I said.

"Whatever."

Jenny got on the back of Koba's Harley, and I followed along on my Rabbit.

By the end of that night I knew where I stood. All of us ended up in the same bed, and I was the odd man out. When I woke up in the morning I was absolutely certain that Koba had had sex with his sister while I was in some kind of alcoholic coma lying right next to them. There they were when I blinked into consciousness, arms wound around each other like newlyweds.

Ernest, you say I just had some bad luck. Bad luck, indeed: One crazy girlfriend and another who liked to fuck her brother. Jenny also had an ambiguous relationship of some kind with her father. This was back when he had been accused of "un-American activities," tried as an accomplice of a Soviet spy, and was about to go off to a Federal penitentiary for twenty years. He was one of those who wouldn't "name names," but he wasn't famous like Arthur Miller. So the McCarthy Committee had no trouble damaging his reputation and cooking up a show trial without kindling any expressions of outrage from well known people. Jenny knew he was about to be put away and wanted, she said, "to make him happy." She would have been about sixteen. I was slowly learning not to be amazed by revelations like this. But what the hell. I was just McRubberband Talbot. I was getting used to the idea that the best possible place for me was going to be deep, deep, deep underground. In an archive. And yet Koba was a real friend and, in spite of everything, in spite of the wild extent of our differences, he continued to drag me along on his vision-quest. And I still thought I was in love with his sister. Things continued to be pretty much the same among the three of us all through 1963 and 1964. But there was no talk of marriage with Jenny. Marriage was something from the 1950s. In the Sixties people "lived together" instead. Can you imagine what that hip generation of literary types would have thought had they been told that even gay and lesbian couples would be clamoring to get married in the next century?

(In passing, Ernest, I ought to note here that it was at about this time I first came across the name of your favorite soon-to-emerge great American fiction-writer, James Walton, whose work I too now revere. There had been a funny mix-up involving the two Richard El(l)man(n)s. Someone sent Richard Ellmann, the Joyce scholar, an annoyed letter saying that he ought to go back to writing literary criticism and biography because his fiction was no good at all. The great academic had no idea that Richard Elman existed, mainly because he had only published a few short stories in fairly obscure little magazines. But he was interested. He asked his graduate assistant at Northwestern to go out and do a little digging, the kind of thing I did for Kerensky, to see if some namesake existed. Walton turned up Kerensky's fellow lodger and Matthias' friend Richard Elman, sent him a letter tactfully explaining the confusion. Elman then began a correspondence with Walton lasting until Elman's death in the 1990s. He showed me the first letter. It was clear, even from the epistolary style, that Walton could write brilliant prose. As yet, however, he was just plodding along on a Conrad dissertation directed by "double l / double n," as Richard the fictionist and his friends called the Northwestern professor.)

My state of mind, locked into a status quo with regard to Jenny and Koba, had begun to lead me not only to value more and more the solitary state of the archivist-at-work, but also to lonely and peripatetic thought in various bucolic Stanford fields, meadows, and glens. They didn't call the place "the farm" for nothing, and there were still plenty of quiet places where the livestock had been withdrawn, the crops replaced by grass and winding footpaths, or where early attempts to communicate with the stars had begun literally and with high hopes. Ernest, you'd have enjoyed the early morning or late evening walks I used to take along the five miles of trails around the famous radio reflector antenna still called "The Dish." I said earlier that the only high-tech equipment that influenced my life in the early 1960s was the Stanford linear accelerator, which shot its small particles directly at my apartment. But I had forgotten The Dish. Unlike the accelerator, its presence was altogether benign. Along with the Hoover Tower, it was the most obvious Stanford landmark. They told us in those days that The Dish was built to monitor nuclear tests, if there were any, way out in the Pacific. But people who worked there made it clear that the real work of Silicon Valley's predecessors was the search for extraterrestrial life. Certain hikers on the paths reported personal encounters with Little Green Men, Chinese sages transported from some early dynasty, or the ancient and anonymous authors of world-famous Noh plays. There were also other rare forms of life, especially the California Tiger Salamander, an amphibian on the endangered species list, for which little creatures Stanford had hired unemployed librarians and English Ph.D.s to build a system of complicated tunnels under streets and highways solely for the purpose of amphibian migration. As for mammals, there were no tigers among the tiger salamanders, but sometimes I would see a mountain lion at some distance and, alas, now and then a mauled sheep or cow. It was the best place to walk that I could find, and a couple of hours up there alone usually served to clear the mind. I could manage to enter a kind of psychological zone where I didn't think about any of the things that were bothering me. It's easier for you to find such a zone, as you've told me many times. A good pipe of new tobacco, a trip out to your garage, and your childhood baseball cards arranged in some kind of invented baseball-solitaire that no one has ever been invited to share. Or sometimes a syntactical analysis of Walton's best and longest sentences.

One night in the early autumn I returned from a solitary walk to find no one at home. I never knew, returning to my apartment now, who might be there: Jenny, Koba, both of them, or one of their friends from somewhere or other who had been given my key and told to make themselves at home. I lay down in my bed and dropped off into a light sleep. Suddenly the phone was ringing. It was my mother.

"How are you, Talbot?" she said. "How's it going?"

"Just the same, Mom. I'm working hard."

"Oh, that's good, that's good."

"Mom, did you call for any particular reason?"

"Well, your father thought I should tell you something, though I don't really think it's all that important."

"Therefore it must be important. What's wrong?"

"Oh, nothing to do with us. We're both just fine, Talbot."

"So? What is it then?"

"Your father thought I should tell you that something's happened to that rabbi he sometimes plays golf with."

I took a deep breath. "Weingarten? What's happened to Rabbi Weingarten?"

"I guess he died," my mother said.

"You *guess* he died?"

"Well, yes. He did die."

"Mother, I really liked Rabbi Weingarten. He was my friend."

"Well, we knew you enjoyed his company now and then, and that's why we thought we should call."

"I don't know what to say. How did he die?"

"Golf ball," said my mother.

"What the hell do you mean *golf ball*?"

"He was hit by one. On the golf course. In the forehead."

"What are you trying to tell me?"

"Just that."

I had a sudden image of Weingarten, hit by some duffer's sharply curving slice from a parallel fairway, taking a few steps, and stumbling into a sand trap. "How did it happen?" I asked.

"Well, there was a player in the foursome headed down a parallel fairway who sliced his shot in such a way that the rabbi was hit in the forehead. He took a couple of steps, and then stumbled into a sand trap. There happened to be a doctor playing in that very foursome who tried to help, but the rabbi died at once. They took him back to the clubhouse on the back of a golf cart. Your father thought you should know."

"I'm going to hang up the phone, Mother. I can't go on talking to you about this."

"Why is that, Talbot?"

"Mother," I said, "you'd never understand."

"Talbot," she said eagerly. "Shall I get in touch with Cora?"

"Please, Mother. Don't even think about it."

"But she knew him too, didn't she? Your"—she paused—"friend?"

"Maybe you should get in touch with Harvey Goldberg."

"He's gone," she said.

"What do you mean he's gone?"

"Left the university. He was hounded last term by the John Birch Society when he became faculty advisor of the Fair Play for Cuba Committee. They packed his lectures and heckled him. He got tired of it and, as I understand it, he had a long-standing offer from Wisconsin. The university there."

"So he's gone to Madison?"

"Is that where the university is? Should I make some inquiries?"

"Mother, I'm putting down the phone." And I did.

I just read on the Google news feed that Philip Roth has stopped writing. This appeared in an interview with the editor of an obscure French "print" journal, so it took a while for it to "go viral." You'll forgive the quotes. My friend Igor Webb told me a while back that Roth was only "shuffling papers" these days. He actually knows Roth, visits him now and then at his isolated home somewhere on Long Island. To me, it seems the equivalent of knowing and visiting Henry James or Edith Wharton. Way beyond my wildest ambitions. But I've been "shuffling papers" too—your own. Here on my desk is the massive manuscript you've left me of Walton's last and unpublished novel, along with an electronic copy I've had scanned into which I've transcribed most of your marginalia. But in absence of any specific instructions from you, save for the mysterious note saying "Please keep this, and keep it in confidence," I'm not at all sure what my responsibilities are. If you hadn't added "and keep it in confidence," I'd just phone Walton—who after all is alive and still lives nearby—and ask him what he'd like me to do with it. We know that he decided against publication. And we know he invented "Ernest Webber" out of things he'd learned from you, which gives you some rights in the matter. Maybe if I just keep talking to you here it will all come clear to me in a while.

So, Ernest, as I come to the point in the story when we actually met, I have to confess that six months after the conversation with my mother I was back—having said goodbye a little too early—in Columbus, living with my parents in the family home. You can imagine how defeated and humiliated I felt. I had simply failed the Stanford final exams, which gave me an experience I'd never had before. It was of course all the fault of Jenny and Koba. Or at any rate Jenny and Koba seemed worthy of blame. They had finally managed to distract me enough that I was inhabiting their world so fully that I forgot to study. Living again in my parents' house meant that I was also not far from Cora, who lived more or less in the same neighborhood. I took care not to be seen around town. I just stayed in the house reading all the books I should have read at Stanford and working on applications for the OSU department of library studies. My parents annoyed me, of course, but I also realized that it wasn't their fault that I'd botched things so badly I'd had to come home with my tail between my legs. I played Klezmer music on my old stereo and discovered a clarinetist I thought was better than Benny Goodman. When my father complained about "all that Jewish music you like so much," I got mad and put on Schoenberg. I had acquired a particular fondness for *Pierrot Lunaire* and the obscure Belgian poet Albert Firaud, out of whose poems, translated into German by the even more obscure Otto Hartleben, Schoenberg concocted his harlequinade through a decadent *dérèglement des sens* achieved by atonality and *Sprechstimme* that suited the spiritual angst I was feeling perfectly. It didn't, however, suit my father's nerves. After a few months of this, he said it was getting to be time "I took my music and moved out."

I really had no one to talk to in Columbus. The rabbi was dead, Cora was out of the question, Goldberg was in Wisconsin. I did go to see Solomon, the archivist, about my application to OSU. He was willing to write me a recommendation and also suggested that I might like to meet his son, Malachi. After Cora and Jenny, I had sworn off girls for good, so I wasn't even considering a social life. Solomon told me that his son was "not my type," but that I might "learn something from him." In fact, Malachi became my roommate for a while.

It was actually *his* room, or apartment, and his father clearly understood that he needed to share the rent with someone. Malachi was broke, wasn't a student, and didn't have a job. I was willing enough to pay half of the modest rent as my father had promised me more than twice what it amounted to if I would leave the house. That left me a good deal. I typed up a form letter, telling people that I'd moved to 2642 Echo Drive, Columbus; telephone, Jefferson 3332. (These were the very last days of such exchanges.) I photocopied the letter and sent it around. A few days after I moved in, the first phone call was from Kerensky.

He'd been out biking with Koba and Elman. Seriously. I have no idea how the whole escapade had come about, but the conversation was like something out of Gogol. He had wanted, he said, to visit "estates" and someone put him in touch with an organization specializing in tours of California wineries and vineyards. But he got the idea that he might better "penetrate" these "estates" on two wheels rather than four, and evidently tried to get in touch with me because he knew about the Rabbit, but discovered that I had left Palo Alto and found himself talking to the dreaded Koba. He and Jenny were still living in my old flat. By that time Elman also had a cycle, and Koba told Kerensky they'd be glad to take him around and could get him a "rental." I had no idea where the "rental" might have come from, but I suspected the Hell's Angels. Before he got around to the purpose of his call, he told me about heading west on Route 1 until they got to the first and oldest winery in the state, "Testal Ruska," as he called it. Testarossa had been a Jesuit seminary, full that day of what turned out to be "deaf poles." I was certain he had said "dead souls." Kerensky wasn't keen on Poles. He also told me, as if I'd care, that he'd lost his "overcoat and nose." The overcoat bit I'd heard correctly, but the other thing he'd lost was the "notes" that were in the overcoat pocket.

"I'b dot a bad ibfuenza, Dalbot, all fum widing on that modocycle wid yur fwiends widout my obercoat," he said.

"I'm sorry about that, Alexander Fyodorovich. Did you visit other wineries?

"Yebsir, dwee more ob dem. All da way down to Camel and da Montaway Pensula. I discover, Dalbod, dat I like de motorbiking and Big Sur."

"You went to Big Sur?"

"Sure. I like it there. Big Sure, I call it; all da girls abailable."

I'm having real difficulty imagining Kerensky on a Harley clinging to the edge of the continent on Route 1 with Koba and Dick Elman leading the way.

"You really did this, Alexander? You're not putting me on?"

"Yebsir. Und your fwind Koba is good guy."

"You actually made peace with Koba?"

"Yebsir."

It seemed now about time to get down to business, so I asked him why he'd phoned. He said he wanted his money back.

"I don't understand, Alexander. What money's that?"

He said it was the part of my salary I hadn't earned, which had all been paid out of his discretionary fund as a visiting scholar. I'd been paid my spring quarter stipend, but then flunked my winter quarter exams and absconded with his money. He'd had cases of expensive wine shipped up from Monterey and then found he lacked the funds to pay an exorbitant rental on his Harley. It was still parked in front of the boarding house he shared with Elman. My first guess had been right, and Koba had obtained a bike from the Angels. Kerensky was scared.

"You know aboud dese Angels, Dalbod, Da?"

"Da," I said.

"You send a check. About three-fifty maybe, Da?"

"I'll send a check. Jenny didn't come along with all of you on the trip?"

"She's looking for you, Dalbot. A dutiful girl."

"I think you mean beautiful."

"Yebsir." He put down the phone.

Malachi was listening to all this and trying to figure out what it was all about. I explained. I also admitted to him that I was giving up women. He said he could understand that, but I doubted that he'd spent any time seriously attached to anyone of the opposite sex. It wasn't that he was gay, he was just gross. To begin with, he chewed gum—lots of it, a great wad in his mouth. His jaw muscles were exaggerated from all the chewing, and he had biceps where his cheeks should have been. It was bubble gum he fancied, the kind you could still get in a flat rectangle with a baseball card. He threw away the baseball cards, but stuffed the entire rectangle of gum in his mouth. It drove me absolutely nuts when I had to prepare for my entrance exams in the library science program. And he blew bubbles. At that point I felt I had a right to object. I'd say, "Look, this gum chewing really bothers me, and I haven't said anything. But blowing bubbles like a six-year-old kid is absolutely beyond my endurance." He said he couldn't help it; it was a habit.

"Is that the same as an addiction?"

"Almost," he said. "I can't not do it."

"Why didn't you warn me about this?"

"I didn't think it was a problem"

He also snored. We had arranged the two-room flat into a double study and a double bedroom. That was a big mistake. During the night, I was kept awake by Malachi's snoring; in the day I had to try and concentrate with the snapping and the bubbling. Now and then we'd have a conversation. It's strange how I began to crave total quiet more than anything. There was a barking dog in the neighborhood that was left out at nights and, after a few weeks, the people living next door began getting a new roof put on. Of course the roofers had a portable radio on which they'd play the loudest rock station in Columbus. And a guy in the alley worked on his car—*rum, rum, rummm, glug glug, glug, sputt sputt.* I shouted up at one of the roofers about the radio, asking him to turn it down. He gave me the finger and turned it up. A day after I complained to the neighbors about their employee's loud radio, I came back to the flat and found the radio, or what had been the radio, broken to pieces on the front porch. It looked like it had been hit with a sledgehammer or a cement block; its entrails were spread all over, along with the bits of its plastic casing. This I took as a death threat.

After several weeks of these minor torments, I headed for the archive and Malachi's dad. I knew it would be quiet there. Solomon was sympathetic. He said he knew his son was "a little rough around the edges," and he perfectly understood about the dog, the roofers, the car mechanic, and the radio. So he offered me a job. He, like Kerensky, seemed to have some kind of discretionary fund. He really didn't care if I worked or not; I'd have a place to study, think, write, or just be quiet. There was even a small cot-like bed I could use after hours if I wanted to. It was in the women's bathroom. "You know," he said, "for the girls when they have their periods and have to lie down." But the whole archive was shut up at night, so no one would find me in the women's loo. "Just make sure you're out of there by 8:00 a.m. if you spend the night." Thus began what I think of as my Bartleby period.

It's not that I never went back to the apartment or ceased to spend any time with Malachi. I found, in fact, that I could tolerate him much more easily once I understood the bolthole was available to me at any time of the day or night. (His father had given me a key.) At first I only used the archive cot when the outside noises were at their worst. Malachi got used to me saying, "Hey, I'll see you in the morning. I think I'm going to go and put in an all-nighter at the library." Refreshed, I'd be quite happy being chummy when I returned in the morning. It seemed that at first he thought I was seeing a girl, so there were some weird winks and nods. But I explained I really enjoyed the odd night of complete silence. It restored me. It cheered me up.

"And you like my old man, right?"

This I acknowledged, saying, "I'm back here to get the credentials that will let me live a life just like his. I got distracted out on the west coast, but now I'm back in control of my life."

"Well," said Malachi, "he's not very much in control of his."

"What do you mean?"

Malachi blew a big bubble with his Stan-the-Man Musial baseball card bubble gum, let it burst, and collected the residue from around his lips and nose with his forefinger.

"Talbot," he said. "The old man is a thief."

That took me aback. He went on to maintain in general terms that any obsessive collector eventually was tempted to theft. Obsessive collecting was an addiction, like lots of other things—like bubble gum, for example. When you couldn't manage to buy something you badly wanted, you found a way to take it. I told him that I found his father an absolutely upright man, in fact a paragon of probity. Malachi shook his head.

"You didn't have him as a father."

Webber, you'll be thinking already that I must have taken a little of Kenneth Cobin's character from this discussion. That's true. The Faulkner scholar in "Westmont and the Bear" doesn't resemble Solomon in his character or personality, but he does resemble him in his "addiction," as Malachi had it. I just hadn't yet had occasion to observe this in Solomon. In fact, I was wholly skeptical at this point and insisted that Malachi give me an example. He said he could give me dozens.

"How about one?"

The story he told me involved the one time that Malachi himself participated in what he called his father's "repeated thefts." He only did it because he was angry himself, for his own reasons, at the people who were to be relieved of something valuable. They happened to be the "brothers" at the OSU Beta Theta Pi fraternity. It was a classy group to be associated with in those days, especially if you wanted girls. Malachi happened to have a high school friend who had become a "Beta" and persuaded his brothers to include Malachi in the fall "rush." At one of the parties at the OSU chapter house, he had been shown a remarkable collection of George Bellows paintings and drawings. Bellows had been a member of the local chapter in his college days. Malachi immediately thought how valuable these works must be, all framed and hung in prominent places around the enormous house. It appeared that Bellows had simply left them behind. Malachi understood at once that his father would be interested in this, as one of his specialties was collecting work that had some association or other with Columbus or Ohio State University. He had accumulated (stolen?) the nation's best collection of James Thurber papers, an achievement that made his early national reputation among his colleagues. Malachi asked the high school friend if there were even more Bellows works that hadn't been framed and hung in the chapter house. There were. At the end of the "rush party" the high school friend showed Malachi drawers full of sketchbooks and notes. After an evening of bubble-gum blowing, Malachi was quickly dropped as a possible Beta "pledge," and he decided he was angry about it. ("You wouldn't believe the girls these guys get.") He was also, he said, a Jewish bubble-gum blower, and he supposed that was part of the problem. At any rate, he told his father about the Beta treasure trove.

"What happened then?"

"I managed to get invited one more time, not to a rush party, but just as a dinner guest. I made friends with the 'house mother.' Do you know what they are? House mothers? They're senile and needy old widows who are paid a salary and given a room in the chapter house. They're a tradition more than a necessity, but all the fraternity houses have one. It gives these places the reputation of discretion while in fact full-scale orgies are going on. The housemothers know perfectly well about all the fucking upstairs; they just shut their apartment doors and turn up the TV. Then they lie on some kind of annual administrative report that gets turned in to university authorities once a year. Anyway, this housemother was a nice old crone and we talked a little about Bellows' work, which she liked. She actually asked me if I'd like to spend some time with what I had seen before in the drawers. After dinner, she took me into the library and left me alone. I filled up my enormous nerdy briefcase with as much as I could fit into it, thanked my hosts for a pleasant time, and took it all to the archive for the old man. I'm sure nobody ever missed what I took. Do you want some more examples?"

I got the picture. Eventually, I admitted to Solomon that his son had filled me in on the cloak and dagger side of archiving, and he told me even

165

better stories himself. He was a good guy, and I liked him. Besides, most of the things he had purloined were better off in the long run there in the archive than in the private hands of greedy family heirs and uninformed nitwits. And Solomon hadn't taken the stuff for himself. These were "Robin Hood thefts," he said, intended eventually for the public good. Or, as Malachi insisted privately to his dad, a symbolic tithing to the annoyed God of his own book of the *Tanakh*. "That's part of your Goy *Old Testament*," Solomon explained, "with all the books in the wrong order, prophets to the rear and *Job* in the middle. Ever read the Hebrew Bible the right way round?" Solomon told me that his son took his name all too seriously: "He likes it that he's named for the last prophet," he said. "He can't even listen to Handel's *Messiah* except autobiographically: *Who shall abide the day of his coming? And who shall stand when he appeareth*, and all that. Now and then he's crazy enough to think it's all about him. Or sometimes he thinks it's all about sex, which he knows about from nothing, Talbot, as you probably know. Watch out what you call your kids. For a while, he got obsessive about people offering 'His Father'— me, that is, in the archive—cheap goods. That's when he agreed to go after the Bellows stuff in that fraternity. It was useful. But look out when he does, actually, start up with his parodic prophesying jive. He's done that now and then, and it really freaks people out. Talks of himself as boss of the Saving Remnant, even with the fucking gum." It was after these revelations that Solomon asked me if I were interested in joining the two of them in some "adventures," but I declined. It turned out to be adventure enough sleeping nights in the women's bathroom.

Slowly enough—it took several months—my Bartleby existence progressed to the extent that I spent less and less time "at home" with Malachi, and more and more time, both days and nights, in the archive. I passed my entrance exams and was once again, though on rather a diminished scale, officially a student of library science. At some point in the middle of the winter—it must have been the winter of 1968, a new year that would lead to the "summer of love" all over the world—that a very confident-seeming young man of about my own age presented himself at the archive and asked if we possibly had anything in the collection by an emerging fiction writer called James Walton. That was you, Ernest Webber.

It's true that the archive actually listed a category called "emerging writers," a rare interest in the rare-books business. Solomon had the idea that if he gathered a lot of chapbooks, broadsides, poster-poems, mimeo magazines, and the like early on he might be making, more or less inadvertently, some good bets on the future. It turned out he was right. The Sixties exploded with small press publications in the same way it did with music, and the archive ended up with valuable collections of a generation that included fiction writers who came after the generation of Roth, Bellow, and Updike: Raymond Carver, Tobias Wolf, T.C. Boyle, Joyce Carol Oates, Robert Coover, the brothers Barthelme, and so on. (Among the poets, Solomon was canny enough to have gotten hold of very early Hass, Peck, and Pinsky—those acquaintances of mine from only the year before—simply by subscribing to *Sequoia*, the Stanford literary magazine.) After looking in the catalogue of new acquisitions, however, I had to tell you that we seemed to have nothing by James Walton. You weren't really surprised, but you were in one of what I later thought of as your "pedagogical moods," so you told me all you knew—and at that point there was very little to know—about the distinguished fiction writer who now happens to live only a mile or so away from me. You recommended, in two Chicago-based little magazines, two of the early stories, "'Tis Enough" and "Loney's Retirement," which we now think of as parts of Walton's first novel, *Margaret's Book*, which to everyone's surprise won the Pulitzer Prize in 1978.

I can't remember what had brought you to OSU from the South Side of Chicago, especially since you had achieved such a distinguished undergraduate record at Northwestern, which was Walton's own university. But it's true, as you told me, that Ohio State had a good English department in those days. You said you didn't want to attend a "high-pressure" grad school. There was someone in particular you wanted to work with, but I can't now remember his name. Anyway, we more or less immediately became friends. I think you were the first entirely sane person I'd become friends with since Joel Barkan in high school. And it didn't take you long to begin worrying about the kind of life I'd been leading. When Solomon came in from his lunch break, I introduced you as "my friend Ernest Webber," and you immediately blushed. But that's the kind of person you were. One could sense your gift of friendship almost at once. Solomon clearly liked you too, and he promised to see what he could find out about James Walton's stories.

By the time we'd finished a wide-ranging free associative conversation in the archive, it was getting on towards happy hour on a Friday afternoon. I phoned Malachi and asked him if he'd like to join us at Larry's, the student watering place directly across the street from my old high school. When Joel Barkan and I were high school seniors, we had been forced to drink what was called "3.2." That meant 3.2 percent alcohol, hardly any alcohol at all, and it was specifically intended for people like us. It took several pitchers of the stuff in order to feel any buzz at all. Everything was different down at Johnny's 402 Club, the jazz joint I've mentioned before. We two white kids were given whatever we wanted. In fact, it amused the black clientele to see us stumbling to our car at the end of a late night of jazz. The music at Larry's was entirely different. My favorite memory, which I told you as we arrived, had to do with the annual "grape stomp" at that venue. An enormous wooden vat full of grapes was somehow assembled in the bar and the full tuba section of the OSU marching band was brought in for the occasion. While the tubas blazed away, patrons took turns dancing among the grapes, barefoot of course, but altogether bare as well. Women's nubile undergraduate bodies were splashed purple in an event that was such a "tradition" that no authority, campus or municipal, sought to interfere with it. Joel and I would sit there, 1958 and 1959, drinking Larry's 3.2 and feasting on the breasts of girls just out of reach, women morphing into Sixties birds before our eyes.

Malachi was there already when you and I arrived. You won't, I'm sure, have forgotten what happened next. I introduced the two of you, we ordered a pitcher of beer, and suddenly I froze. You both could see that something was wrong.

"Hey, Talbot—anything amiss?" asked Malachi.

You smiled sympathetically, pouring a glass of beer for yourself from the enormous common pitcher.

"Look!" I said, pointing to a booth on the opposite side of the room.

There sat Cora and Jenny, chatting casually as if they'd known each other since childhood. I hadn't seen Cora at all since I first left Columbus for Palo Alto. And Jenny I hadn't seen since I left Palo Alto for Columbus. What was going on? I remember that Kerensky had said something about how Jenny had been "looking for me."

"I think I've got to get out of here," I said.

You looked at me quizzically: "Why's that?"

Malachi followed my gaze to the booth: "I think those girls have got designs on him," he grinned, taking a long draught of beer.

"Designs?" you said.

"He's not wrong to want out of here," said Malachi. "Shall I tell you what I think? All of it's bad news, all of it foreseen by me, Malachi. Abomination is committed in the town Ohio hallowed and her covenant's betrayed. Did you know my *Tanakh* scroll gives God a fleeting aspect of the feminine? And Talbot's not the tenderfoot he seems to be."

"What's he saying?" you asked politely.

"Sorry, Ernest," I said. "Do you think you could finish this pitcher with Malachi? I really do have to leave. Come by the archive sometime soon and I'll explain."

I didn't actually see you again for a couple of weeks. But in fear of whatever that conversation between Jenny and Cora might portend, I finally settled into the women's bathroom adjacent to the archive as a permanent nighttime residence, bringing in various pills and soaps and toiletries from the apartment. If Malachi didn't give me away, no one but you would know where I was as I tried to think through what I should do about Jenny and Cora.

Obviously, I could have taken the direct approach—phoned Cora at her home or Koba out in Palo Alto who was presumably still living in my old flat. But there seemed a certain amount of risk in that. I might even have phoned Kerensky. The fact that these two women had somehow managed to get together in Columbus boggled my mind. What could explain it? Jenny certainly wasn't the kind of person to chase someone like me all across the country, and, although she was pretty crazy herself, she wasn't as crazy as Cora and wouldn't, I'd have thought, have enjoyed being around her at all. As far as I knew, they had only exchanged a few words, and those more than a year before during that telephone call the night when Cora phoned me and Jenny admitted that she was "the new girlfriend." Anyway, I decided just to lie low. I borrowed a fedora from Solomon and wore it pulled down over my eyes when I went to class. When not in class, I worked in the archive away from the front desk. Malachi had clued-in his old man, so Solomon understood. When the library closed for the night, I took my books and shaving kit into the women's loo and settled in for the night. I spent a lot of time reading alone.

I was, in fact, able to read those two Walton stories you had been raving about when Solomon got them, quite quickly, from a dealer who was able to find magazines as obscure as *The Canalport Intelligencer* and *The South Side Anarchist*. These journals printed the stories that were interpolated eventually in *Margaret's Book*. They were brilliantly written, but very depressing. The first was about a village idiot—"mentally-challenged adult"—who was bullied by some tough kids who stole his baseball cards and meager evening's supply of groceries as he walked home from a shop, then beat him up in an abandoned building and stabbed him with a long shard of broken glass. The other one, much longer, dealt with a retired community college teacher called Loney—Walton's characters have that kind of name—whose isolation and self-absorption lead him to think that the unpleasant son of the old lady living on the first floor of his house is plotting his mother's murder. When the stories finally appeared in the context of *Margaret's Book*, they were read aloud to a kind of conjured ghost-auditor, Margaret, by the "author," Preston Belcher. Again, those names! When Belcher visits one of the Canalport bars he's greeted indifferently by two regulars as he takes a seat beside them: *Hey, Belch; Hiya, Belch*. But I don't need to tell you about the stories since I was reading them because you yourself had recommended them and already knew them well.

You did in fact drop by the archive a week or so after the Cora and Jenny sighting at Larry's. You were perfectly happy drinking cups of stale coffee with me in the back room and catching me up with what was going on in the outer world. But I could tell, too, that you intended to tempt me out of my Bartleby hiding place in all due course. Your approach to my eccentricity was to take my whole situation as a really terrific joke. That a "man of my age" was actually afraid of two beautiful women, both of whom seemed to be on his trail, you thought was "really a great shame." Why hadn't I just introduced him to the ladies, giving Malachi the ditch, so that all four of us might have gone out for the evening? I explained that things were all mixed up with people like the dead rabbi, Harvey Goldberg, Koba, and Alexander Kerensky.

"Alexander Kerensky?" you said, laughing.

So I told you that part of my recent past. You loved it, especially the part about Kerensky's phone call after the biking episode with Koba south on California's costal Route 1. But the Koba and Jenny bit disturbed you. You have something of a traditional moralist in you, old boy, and you said in no uncertain terms: "Any kind of incest is always a terrible thing. I hope it stops." You were/are also, I discovered, quite touchy on the question of ethics with regard to the use of people's actual lives in what passes for fiction, and you were rather horrified that someone might even be tempted to retain the real names of those people in a story or novel (as I have here). If they were "public figures," you thought, they were fair game because they had surrendered part of their privacy voluntarily. But it was quite terrible to raid a friend's life without his permission and take from him something that was inalienably his own alone. My position on the question was complicated then, essentially being that it all depended on a) the nature of the relationship and b) the quality of the writing. Henry James, for example, was welcome to whatever he wanted. And so, when you got down to it, was Walton. Strange thing is, of course, that he eventually wanted a part of you.

Another good talk we had in the early days had to do with my chosen profession, which you thoroughly approved of. This was a relief, after years of dealing with people who saw it as a joke. You believed early on that something fundamental was going to happen to the printed word with the closing of the great and by you (somewhat prematurely) lamented Gutenberg era. You believed that "whatever comes next" would mean that books, especially things like novels, would slowly cease to exist and therefore needed to be collected and saved, just as manuscripts had been saved by the medieval monasteries. In fact, resisting the Bartleby nickname, you began quite early calling me Monk Talbot and, when you didn't quite like the rhythm of that, changed it to Monkey Talbot, which I became. Monkey Talbot, for God's sake! But what you predicted of course has come true. I can't, for example, find a single one of your own books available in "hard copy" in any kind of generalized computer "search" as I flip back and forth from this page to the Internet and back. But when I go to our own internal pages, which have not yet gone public "on line," I find every scrap, published and unpublished, that you've left behind electronically here in our little college collection. But even that's nothing to what pops up when I type in "Ernest Webber/James Walton." With that I get to see—and this was your intention—electronic pages of Walton's last, greatest, but unpublished and maybe unpublishable work, *The History of Romance,* in which you appear as a character, along with the marginal notes I long ago transcribed myself. Your name appears in red, while all the rest of the text is black, and I'm only shown the pages on which it appears. There are strange gaps, therefore, in the narrative. But there you are, as Browning wrote of the murdered duchess in the painting, "as if alive."

As if alive, we got to know each other pretty quickly back there in the archive's depths. I told you of course about my initial adventures in the locked porno room when I was still an undergraduate and still fucking crazy Cora. And you told me about your early life in Canalport and Chicago's South Side. And about how you heard something of Walton's early reputation hanging out with White Sox fans among the losers who frequented bars with Cubs pennants hanging on the walls. They knew him only as an unimpeachable source of baseball statistics, but they'd heard he wrote stories. Years later, sitting in the same bars, you heard the baseball fans remarking that the gossip was he'd stopped. Walton, that is. Had stopped writing stories. But they claimed to have heard as well that there was one last unpublished book, and that "all of us are in it." Well, they were right. There's one last novel, but, aside from you, I'm the only person who has ever read it.

When I call up "annotated version" I find the notes that I carefully transcribed from your ballpoint marginalia to the elegant, clear blue rectangles that you see, just to the right of the text. And, of course, I can make them disappear again by mousing a click on "un-annotated version." (What ingenious changes since old Solomon's day.) Many of your notes have to do with parts of *Margaret's Book* that are absorbed and revised in *A History of Romance*. And, of course you're particularly attentive to any appearance of "Ernest Webber" in the text. You come back again and again to a passage that Walton took from Preston Belcher in *Margaret's Book* and gave to you—I mean to "Ernest Webber"—in the unpublished work. This, after all, was part of the sermon you preached to me, your argument that too much had already been written and that our only task was really preservation. But he also puts in Webber's mouth what must have been the main reason he himself stopped writing. Authors as different as Chaucer and Rimbaud have renounced writing over the ages, but Ernest Webber's reasons (and before that Preston Belcher's and so clearly also Walton's own), had a kind of attractive modesty.

And so Walton takes what Preston said to the spectral Margaret and gives the speech to Webber. It's still the answer to Margaret's question, "why won't you go on? There's so much you could accomplish." But Webber says, like Preston: "People like us"—and I'm sure that includes people like me—"mustn't try to accomplish and shine and impress. That was for the 'great,' who are always in some way also the mad, and who became the morbid and often sordid sum of their accomplishments. People like us think too much of what a *whole life* might add up to. We spend so much time among the great—the great minds, great imaginations, great *wills*—that we can't think of our life as worth anything unless we get some of that greatness for ourselves. But Charlotte Brontë and Thackeray; Dickens and even George Eliot; Henry James and Joyce; these were not 'good' people. If we knew them personally we wouldn't like them. Their personalities would leap out at us like *tigers*." You've circled the passage in the manuscript and written in the margin: "This is not quite what I said, and W. has twisted it in order to make it work. Since he absorbs everything he hears, best to let him do the talking." But I think this is pretty much the gist of what you said to me one night in the OSU archive. Along with your jocular and habitual goodbye when you left me: "Just you keep on collecting, Mr. Monkey."

Well, that I did, and here I am, still at the little college where we both ended up being employed and then stayed on for years and years.

But I should cut to the chase, or maybe better the hide-and-seek. As I slowly became accustomed to living in the archive, I became a little careless. Instead of making certain that I was already there at closing time, I'd arrive late and have to use Solomon's key. Now and again I'd see someone giving me a quizzical look as I went in the library just as everyone else was coming out. One time, arriving after midnight, I was afraid I'd gotten stuck in the elevator, or that its machinery had gone a little crazy. The archive was on the twelfth floor. On this particular night, I pushed 12 only to have the elevator jerk to a halt just after it had started up. When I was on the verge of pressing the "emergency" button, it started up again, but stopped on the second floor. The door opened and nobody was there. The same thing happened on the third floor, the fourth, the fifth, and all the way up to the twelfth, where I was finally able to get off. Was this a mechanical glitch of some kind, or was someone messing me around?

There were other things I couldn't explain to my satisfaction. An entire box of James Thurber papers I'd been working on disappeared from my desk. I couldn't admit to Solomon that I'd misplaced them, so I looked all over for a couple of days, finally finding them in the porn room. But who would have left them there. It was a part of the archive I no longer had any interest in visiting. Another time, I found a baseball card, the kind that came with Malachi's rectangles of bubble gum, used as a bookmark in a rare edition of Booth Tarkington's *The Magnificent Ambersons*. (Tarkington, of course, was the name that you, Ernest, suggested for the college where Westmont works in "Westmont and the Bear" when my original name seemed to you a little too close to that of our own Midwestern halls of ivy.) When I next saw Malachi, I asked him if he'd been hanging around the archive himself or had taken an interest in Midwestern fiction. He said he hadn't and, when I told him about the baseball card, he suggested that I'd probably used it as a bookmark in a book "at home" and slipped it into the *Ambersons* without quite realizing it. This was plausible, since the baseball cards were everywhere "at home."

At this date, there was of course no such thing as a telephone message machine. There were primitive reel-to-reel tape recorders, and there were dictaphones. Both of these contraptions seemed marvelous enough as technology. But any messages were taken down by the archive secretary and left in our pigeonholes. I got a few weird ones. Someone "who wouldn't give a name" left a message saying, as if it were a newspaper headline, "Harassment rate increases locally." A few days later there was another: "Memory is the mother of invention." Then a third: "Phony names for real dames." I of course asked the secretary if any of this made sense to her. She said, "I just work here, Mr. Eastmore."

One dark and stormy night I got in really late, after two a.m. I'd been out with you, Ernest, listening to a concert by the Columbus Symphony which had taken over the RKO Palace movie theater where I had seen "firstrun movies" when I was a kid. I think it was the first Shostakovich I'd ever heard, the 7th symphony, "about" the siege of Leningrad. It got a mixed response from the audience: none of the local Republicans who thought they must support "culture" because of their wives, were sure whether they should like the 7th because it was anti-Nazi or dislike it because it was pro-Soviet. Hello, Columbus! Anyway, after the concert we'd gone to an all-night coffeehouse and were talking politics. I told you about Harvey Goldberg's leftist oratory in his classroom. You told me about your uncle, a Chicago mafia type who'd worked with one of Capone's "associates." I told you about the Fair Play for Cuba Committee in 1962. You told me what it was like getting a bill through Mayor Daly's City Council. We were talking about different things. So was Shostakovich. When we realized it was getting really late, you drove me to the library, where we said goodbye. Since it was past closing time for the library as a whole, not just the archive, I had to use a second key that Solomon had given me to open the outer door and let myself in. Once inside, I took the elevator up to the twelfth floor without any mechanical mishaps. When I used my second key to open the door of the archive, I had the distinct sense that I was smelling smoke, marijuana in fact, and smoking of any kind was of course strictly prohibited anywhere in the archive. Without even looking around for the source of the smoke, I used my third key to let myself into the women's bathroom. And there were Cora and Jenny, sitting together on the bed and looking up at me, smoking their reefers: "Hi there, Talbot, Cora said. I think you already know my friend." I did.

But I don't know what to do next. The problem is that having written this much I don't know any longer what happens. Once I thought I did. The whole process of thinking and writing was suddenly disrupted by a single phone call, not in 1968, but in 2012. We had been out together in our little college town, "Tarkington village" I called it in the Westmont stories you'd read, and we'd had a good dinner in what one always told visitors was "the only decent restaurant in town," just the place one would take a distinguished guest, whether Phillip Roth or Robert Hass. You told me you'd been to your doctor recently to check out your "smoker's cough." You'd worried about that before, so neither of us dwelt on what might be a bad report. We talked about a lot more that night than we usually did, more even than in that long conversation following the Shostakovich in Columbus. Our talk had something elegiac about it, but we were perfectly cheerful, even kind of carefree, in spirit. We laughed a lot, often at ourselves. We nattered on about the foolishness, in all of its manifestations, of the academic life. About the pleasures of a good meal, and a good wine to go with it; about beautiful women, how excellent they are; about Henry James, especially the late Henry James, *The Ambassadors, Wings of the Dove, The Golden Bowl*; about people who had inspired us, in my case Harvey Goldberg and Rabbi Weingarten, in your case Richard Ellmann at Northwestern; about batters and catchers and short stops, players you knew as well as your nearest relatives and about whom I had heard nothing at all; about children, which neither of us had, but nonetheless thought entirely beautiful; about politicians, how wicked they are and how we were sorry that nothing got better after the Vietnam years; about how we hoped nonetheless that things might get better in the future; about great lines in great poems; about the work of the Anglo-Welsh poet David Jones from whom I'm taking these rhythms and about whom almost nobody knows any more; about how all the good causes are probably lost causes; about the new Mayor in our poor little town, Pete Buttigieg, and about how much we liked him; about Philip Roth's *Goodbye, Columbus* and my friend Koba and his sister Jenny; about how Roth really didn't know anything at all about Columbus, Ohio; about my dead mother and father; about your own dead mother and father; about the stories I'd written about a character called "Westmont," and about how bad they were; about the fact that you liked them anyway; about a certain walk by the river which we had both taken, but only alone by ourselves; about the "Council Oak" in the city cemetery, which had been the place where Potawatomies negotiated with La Salle; about the cemetery itself, where we both thought we'd eventually end up if someone bothered to bury our ashes; about old friends, especially those of each whom the other had never met; about what we'd called "the revolution" in the sixties; about how little anyone in the sixties understood about such terrifying upheavals; about Shostakovich, his music; about trying to save what's worth being saved; about how difficult it is to know what is and what's not worth being saved; about archives; about archivists; about me; about you…

The next afternoon you phoned. You'd had the results of the CT scan and, early in the morning, an MRI. You said: "I'm not authorizing any treatment."

"What do you mean?"

"It's terminal, Talbot."

I couldn't say anything for a moment, and I admit I thought about this unfinished story. Unregenerate! Stupid, petty, and vain. But you brought it up yourself.

"That story you gave me," you said. "You don't know where to go next, do you my friend."

I said that hardly mattered anymore.

"Yes, it does," you said. "I'm only a character in James Walton's novel myself. I mean from now on."

"I know that," I said.

"Well," you said. "Why don't you leave it just the way it is? You asked my advice, after all, and that's my advice. I'll be pretty dead pretty soon, and that gives me a kind of authority, don't you think?"

"It does, Ernest, it does."

"If you wanted really professional advice, you could always give Walton a call. He might not want to talk about it, though. He's given this sort of thing up, as you know. But he's kind and polite, so if you asked him he'd probably help."

"I don't think I'll ask him, Ernest."

"The main thing is not to ask him anything about *The History of Romance*. That's between you and me and the archive now."

"Understood."

"He was serious, you know, about what he said in *Margaret's Book*."

"I know he was."

"You'll be surprised that I wish you had married Cora or Jenny. They were both beautiful women."

"Ernest," I said. "They existed only in fiction."

"What's the difference?" you said. And then you laughed: "At my stage of life, anyway. So I'll take back some of those gripes I aired to you about what Walton did with my life. I kind of like it now, I have to confess, since it exists just among the three of us. But I do wish you'd married. You're lonely, like Loney in *Margaret's Book*."

"I gave Westmont a wife in 'Westmont and the Teapot.'"

"Indeed you did. A funny story, Talbot."

I couldn't think of what else to say. "Ernest?" I said.

"What is it, Talbot?"

176

I thought, but didn't say, that I would probably want to re-read all those pages about him in Walton's book again and again in years to come. Slowly, as he seemed to know, those words and those words alone would constitute the real "Ernest Webber."

"Ernest," I said. "I can't think of anything else to say."

"Oh, that's okay, Talbot," you said. "That's entirely okay with me."

Westmont and the Different Kinds of Music

6

Because he was so exclusively a jazz fan from an early age, Westmont missed Elvis Presley entirely. Stubbornly, he also missed Peter, Paul and Mary, early Bob Dylan, the Beatles, the Rolling Stones, later Bob Dylan, The Doors, the Grateful Dead, and so on. However, he did not miss Gustav Mahler. During his junior year in college, he was offered a free ticket to hear, in Columbus, Ohio, of all places, the Berlin Philharmonic playing Mahler's 5th symphony, conducted by Herbert von Karajan. In Columbus von Karajan (a former Nazi) was received as a cultural icon representing Freedom, West Berlin, Capitalism, and any number of things other than music. Westmont didn't care. When the tears poured down his cheeks during the *adagio* movement, he was embarrassed, but also in a state of aesthetic bliss. It wasn't that he immediately gave up Dave Brubeck, Thelonious Monk, Miles Davis, John Coltrane, or Gerry Mulligan. More that he began slowly to drift away from jazz. His collection of LPs was soon about fifty percent classical, as he moved both forward and back in time—a Handel oratorio one day, a piece by Stravinsky or Bartók the next. When he met the woman who would eventually become (for a little while) his wife, he was astonished to discover that she was born ten miles away from where Benjamin Britten had founded his music festival, in Aldeburgh, Suffolk. At that very moment Britten's *War Requiem* had become his favorite piece of music. He had listened again and again to the first LP recording of the piece—the one with Peter Pears, Dietrich Fischer-Dieskau, and Galina Vishnevskaya. It was conducted by Britten himself. His future wife's mother knew people like Myfanwy Piper (librettist) and Lord Harewood (patron and friend of Britten and his partner, the tenor Peter Pears). Although he could not pronounce either Myfanwy or Vishnevskaya, Westmont was delighted to find someone who liked the same kind of music that he himself was beginning to revere. She asked him early on what instrument he played. He was abashed that he had to say none. But she liked him anyway, and they were married in an Episcopal church where the organist was paid an extra fee to learn Britten's "Hymn to Saint Cecelia" and train a children's choir. After living with Westmont in a small college town where he became head archivist, his wife returned to England for a long stay and Westmont cautiously started listening again to Monk and Miles Davis, then tried some CD versions of old LPs by the Grateful Dead, the later Dylan, the early Dylan, and even read a book by a literary scholar comparing Jim Morrison of The Doors with the French *poète maudit*, Arthur Rimbaud.

Westmont and the Different Kinds of Music

Epilogue

When his wife suddenly returned from England, Timothy Westmont was half asleep listening to Schubert's Quintet, D956, played on an old CD by the Juilliard String Quartet with Bernard Greenhouse as the second cello. In his extreme old age—80 now, which was not, as his former interns liked to joke, "the new sixty"—Schubert's quintet had become his favorite music of all, especially the stark and intimate *adagio* movement that sometimes moved him so deeply that he dared not listen all the way to the end but pushed the remote before it had finished to advance the contraption quickly on to the *scherzo*. He had listened to the piece hundreds of times, though Schubert himself hadn't lived to hear it performed even once...

...Westmont's wife was suddenly there, in his house, in her house, in the music. She had given him no warning at all of her imminent arrival. She simply opened the door, which he had neglected to lock, and stood there smiling. Westmont awoke from his daze and stared at her, somehow not really surprised. His wife closed the door behind her, and even clicked the latch of the deadbolt, before turning again to face her husband. It had been more than a decade since they had seen each other. Westmont thought she looked younger than he would have expected, though quite frail and perhaps not well. The *adagio* movement started to play... *welche aus dem Kunstlied geboren ist, das Ganze durchdringt... Born of song, a strain of painful lyricism, love...* It was a *Deutsche Grammophon* recording, and he had inadvertently memorized the German jacket notes, modifying and expanding them in English as an archivist's scholarly gloss. He was like that. He couldn't help himself.

"Such sad music," Westmont said, standing up and looking at his wife where she still stood just inside the door, somehow conjured there by Schubert.

"It's beautiful," she said. "It makes me happy."

*The final eleven bars of the second movement of
Schubert's Quintet in C major (D. 956, Op. posth. 163), 1828.*